THE LORD'S COMPASS

THE RECKLESS ROGUES
BOOK FOUR

ELLIE ST. CLAIR

♥ **Copyright 2023 Ellie St Clair**

All rights reserved.

This book or parts thereof may not be reproduced in any form, stored in any retrieval system, or transmitted in any form by any means—electronic, mechanical, photocopy, recording, or otherwise—without prior written permission of the publisher.

Facebook: Ellie St. Clair

Cover by AJF Designs

Do you love historical romance? Receive access to a free ebook, as well as exclusive content such as giveaways, contests, freebies and advance notice of pre-orders through my mailing list!

Sign up here!

Reckless Rogues
The Earls's Secret
The Viscount's Code
The Scholar's Key
The Lord's Compass
The Heir's Fortune

For a full list of all of Ellie's books, please see
www.elliestclair.com/books.

CHAPTER 1

1806 ~ KENT, ENGLAND

*E*ric had no idea where he was going.

Did he own this estate? Yes, in a sense. It was one of a few that his family had obtained over the many years of the storied Rowley history that his father had been so keen on sharing with him. Eric, however, did not need multiple estates and therefore had gifted it to his brother and his new bride as it was perfect for Noah.

It was not as though Eric had ever spent a great amount of time here. He had grown up on his family's entailed estate, Hollingsworth. He was lord there now that his father had passed, although his mother ran the place. He knew he should take on the responsibility but, the truth was, it was far easier for him this way.

He wondered now if these gardens he found himself in were supposed to be a maze, or if the hedges had grown that way over time.

He had no idea how to return to the festivities. He

supposed if he wandered long enough, he'd eventually find his way back.

His brother's wedding had occurred just that morning, and Eric had never seen Noah as happy as he was today.

Despite the bride and groom disappearing for a time, the small party had continued the marriage celebrations, led by Eric himself until he had decided to take to the gardens to smoke his cheroot away from everyone else as the ladies were not fond of the smoke.

Then a little wandering had led to his current situation.

"How in the hell did I end up here?" he mused, scratching his temple and turning around in a circle. He looked up, seeing the house rising in the distance, seemingly grinning down at him mockingly. It should be... north? Directions had always confused him. He had tried multiple times now to make his way toward the house and reached a dead end with every attempt.

Suddenly he heard a snap and a whistle right next to his ear before an arrow hit a target — one he had not noticed until now — ahead and to the right of him with a *thud*. He had enough wherewithal to observe that it lodged directly in the center.

"Having trouble?"

He whirled around at the voice, both surprised and pleased to find Lady Faith Embury standing twenty yards away across the grass, watching him with mirth in her blue eyes, her face, with its high cheekbones and well-defined jawline, otherwise expressionless, her arms crossed through a bow in front of her.

"Not at all," he said, lifting his chin. "Simply enjoying some afternoon air."

"I can smell the smoke from here," she said, wrinkling her nose, and Eric would have laughed if he wasn't awestruck by her presence. She was a tall woman, as strong physically as she was within, but she held herself with such confidence that he had never been able to resist the pull toward her – one that now caused him some vexation.

He threw down the nearly finished cheroot and extinguished it with his foot, snapping his heel before clasping his hands behind his back and walking toward her.

"Did you need a break from all of your dancing?" she asked, tilting her head to the side, her smile as brittle as the sarcasm that dripped from her words.

"You were watching me?" he asked with a grin that he knew would only serve to annoy her, but he couldn't seem to help himself from pestering her.

She shifted slightly from one foot to the other, enough to show that he had irked her, and he couldn't contain his pleasure that he had achieved his goal.

"You're rather hard to miss, the way you flit from woman to woman," she said, lifting her nose in the air. "Half the women in there are married. Or does that not concern you?"

He reached out and took her bow, running his fingers over the fine wood as he examined it, wishing it was her soft skin he was touching so intimately instead.

"You're jealous."

"I am most certainly not!" she said hotly, crossing her arms over her chest as though warding him away.

"Believe that if you want," he said, leaning down and tucking a piece of her dark blond hair behind her ear. "But we both know the truth."

"You're impossible," she said, turning her head to the side.

"Not impossible. I am correct. Always am on these things," he said, reaching out to tap her nose, and she slapped his hand away.

"Do not touch me."

"I thought you liked it when I touched you."

"I did once. But that was before."

"Before what?" he asked, genuinely wanting to know. He had waited two years to learn what had caused her interest in him to suddenly turn to such disdain.

"You know very well to what I am referring."

"Actually," he retorted, "I do not. Are you ready to talk about our kiss yet or do you need another year or two?"

She whipped her head from one side to the other as though to make sure that no one could hear them, and Eric couldn't help but chuckle.

"I doubt there is anyone within hearing distance. What *are* you doing out here alone shooting arrows during a party, anyway?"

He knew how much she enjoyed archery, and while they had all participated in the sport yesterday, now was rather odd timing for it.

"I wanted to be alone."

"You are not exactly dressed for shooting," he said, using his words as an excuse to run his eyes up and down her body, appreciating her lean form and the strength in her arms.

"My attire is none of your concern. As it happens, I am surprised you would remember our... kiss. Is such an act not a frequent occurrence in your life?" she asked, raising a brow, but he could tell that she was interested in his answer – and slightly flustered at this turn of conversation, if the pinkish hue rising in her cheeks was any indication.

"I am not the rake you think I am."

"No?"

"Not at all."

"Then why does every woman who mentions your name do so with a smile on her face and a twinkle in her eye?" she asked, the hostility remaining.

"Because of my wit and charm," he said, grinning again, as he loved teasing her.

"Mm-hmm."

She turned in a swirl of silver skirts, picked up her quiver and walked over to the target, from which she plucked five arrows, all gathered near the center. At least now he had a better idea of where he was. How had he not recognized the course? He really must be more observant.

"Are you ready to return?" he asked, and, despite her height, she still had to tilt her head back to look up at him, her crystal blue eyes vibrant beneath her lashes.

Suddenly they blinked and looked around them before returning to his face.

"You are lost," she said, the realization dawning, the first hint of a smile tugging at her lips. "You do not know how to return, do you?"

"Of course I do!" he said indignantly. "I own this place. At least, I did until recently."

"And yet you cannot find your way back." She let out a slight chuckle of glee.

"I can."

"Prove it."

"What?"

"Prove that you know how to return to the house," she said, stepping closer to him.

"How do you suggest I do that?"

"Very simply. Lead us back," she said, waving her arm forward. "I am ready to return."

She lifted the quiver of arrows onto her back and slid the bow over her arm.

"I'll carry those for you," he said, holding his hands out.

"It's fine."

"No," he said with a pointed stare. "It is not. How would it look if I returned with you carrying everything and me alone?"

Her mirth quickly took a turn to annoyance once more. "That is your concern? How it would look to others?"

Goodness, she was beautiful when she was all fired up like this. He just wished it wasn't in such anger towards him. She hadn't always been like this. She used to be much sweeter and would allow him lenience she didn't to any others. But everything had changed between them now, and the vibrant charm of before had transformed into ire that always appeared to be directed toward him.

"Just give me the bag," he said, holding his arm out, and she reluctantly slid it off her shoulders and passed it to him.

"It's called a quiver."

"I know."

He set his feet toward the house and paused, looking over to her, needing her to lead but determined not to tell her so.

She rolled her eyes and shook her head. "This way," she said, pointing down the path to the right.

"I know the way."

"Lord Ferrington, everyone knows that you should not be out wandering alone. I wish you would realize it as well."

"I am not a child."

"Are you not?"

"No," he said indignantly, "of course not."

For the first time, however, her words unsettled him. For as rude as she had been to him over the past two years, they had never had the opportunity for such a long conversation alone. She had made sure of it.

Now that they had, he wondered if their relationship should have remained as it had been – distant.

* * *

FAITH HATED how much he disconcerted her.

As he walked beside her, her quiver on his back, she became increasingly annoyed at how much his presence affected her.

There was a good few feet between them, and yet it seemed as though she could sense the heat from his body radiating across the short distance. He had always had such magnetism. It was more than the size of his body. It was the way he carried himself, the heartiness of his laughter, his ability to say what he thought without restriction.

He was everything she wanted to be.

And everything she could have had if only things had been different.

But the man he was – the flirt, the charmer – was the very reason they were not together. For she was selfish. She didn't like sharing – most especially him.

Which was why she tried to distance herself from him, for seeing him with other women only made everything worse.

"I know where we are now," he said as they turned onto the path toward the house.

"I should hope so," she said wryly. "This takes you straight to the terrace."

"Where would you like me to take your bow and arrows?"

"I can take them from here," she said, holding out her hands, but he shook his head, his dark hair, too long for the style of the day, but of course annoyingly charming on him, sliding over his forehead.

"I am far too much of a gentleman to allow you to do so."

"Oh, you are a gentleman now?"

"Always have been," he said jovially, his devilish dimples deepening. "That's what the title of earl gets you."

She shook her head at his cheek and turned toward the stables. "One of the stableboys can take care of them," she said, and he followed.

"As you wish," he said. "Now tell me, why did you leave the party?"

"I am not much one for parties," she said, keeping her

gaze ahead so that he wouldn't read the lie in her eyes. But the truth was far worse – for the truth was, she hadn't been able to stop herself from watching him flirt with Percy's cousin, Lady Rebecca.

It had tugged at her heart, especially after what she had thought was a moment between her and Eric during the wedding ceremony. As her closest friend, Lady Persephone Holloway, had married Eric's brother, Noah, Faith had stood beside her as her bridesmaid while Eric had been his best man. She hadn't been able to take her eyes off of Eric as the clergyman read the words tying the married couple together.

And she had hated herself for it.

Of course, to him a longing gaze was nothing.

She was a fool.

But she had known that for some time.

"I remember one party you seemed to particularly enjoy," he said, wiggling his eyebrows.

Her spine stiffened. "You think quite highly of yourself, Lord Ferrington," she said tersely.

"Faith, there is no need to be so formal."

"There are many reasons to be formal, my lord."

"Faith—"

"Lady Faith."

He sighed, the first sign of his cheeriness slipping.

"Lady Faith, then."

He stopped as they neared the stables, turning to stand in front of her. His full lips were pressed into a line as his hazel eyes stared into hers. "What happened, Faith? What changed?"

She stared at him. She had told herself she would never speak of this, but perhaps this is what she needed – what they both needed to close this door.

"I saw you with her."

He flinched backward at the intensity of her tone, although his mask of confession remained. "With whom?"

"The other woman. That night."

"Faith, I do not know who you mean, there was no—" He stopped abruptly, his eyes widening as, apparently, his memory restored itself. "Another woman… you saw that?"

"I did," she said, stepping forward, snatching her quiver from his grasp, which had slackened in his surprise at her revelation. "Which is why there will never be such thing as you and me again."

CHAPTER 2

"What has you so glum?"

Eric looked up at Whitehall and couldn't help a humorless chuckle at the irony of Whitehall asking such a question.

"Nothing."

"Come now – Eric Rowley is nothing but jovial. There can only be one explanation."

Eric lifted an eyebrow and waited.

"A woman."

Eric sighed and threw his head back dramatically. "You are not wrong, my friend."

Whitehall tapped one finger against his arm as he scanned his gaze across the company gathered within the drawing room, which included the Rowley family, which was rather small – only Eric, Noah, and their mother – as well as Lady Percy's parents, her brother and his betrothed, her aunt and uncle and cousins, and the close-knit friends that had become like family.

"Let me see," Whitehall said, stroking his chin as he continued to cast his eyes around the room. "Who could it

THE LORD'S COMPASS

be? Better not be Hope, as she is my wife. Covington's wife is about to have his child which would be a bit much, even for you. It is Lady Percy's wedding day and she is marrying your brother. Could it be Lady Madeline? No, she is much too forceful a woman for you. Then there are Lady Percy's cousins—"

"No need to be reticent," Eric said, rolling his eyes. "You know who it is. You all do."

"Lady Faith."

"Yes."

Whitehall fixed him with a gaze. "I am not one to question another's affections, and while my dear sister-in-law has grown on me since I first met her, Faith is rather prickly – most especially toward you. I cannot quite understand why you are so hell-bent on pursuing her."

"I wish I knew, Whitehall," Eric said, shaking his head sadly. "I wish I knew."

He also wished she had allowed him to explain himself, but as soon as she had plucked the quiver from his hands, she had marched into the stables, refusing to turn around when he called out her name. He had tried to follow her, but he knew creating a scene in front of all the servants within the stables would only make everything worse.

"Can't say I like this side of you."

"No?" Eric tilted his head toward his friend. "Thought you, of anyone, would appreciate it."

Whitehall snorted. "Well, it seems I prefer when you balance me out. There can only be so much melancholy in one room."

"Ferrington, melancholy?" They both turned toward Ashford, who had just joined them. Eric felt a bit of a kinship with Gideon Sutcliffe, for he was now the only other gentleman within their company of friends who remained unmarried. He also held the responsibility for his family and the title. His father, while alive, had lost the mental capacity to look after it all. Unfortunately, Ashford hadn't stepped in until after his father had lost nearly the entirety of their fortune.

Which was exactly why Eric had promised to undertake this journey.

"Never melancholy for any length of time," Eric said, forcing a smile onto his face. It was so frequently present that it appeared rather easily. "A glass of brandy and I shall be myself again."

"You'll be out of luck there," Covington said, hearing the last of Eric's words as he joined them. "I am fairly certain the ladies have drunk it all."

"I'm sorry, I thought I just heard you say that the *ladies* drank it all," Eric said, turning toward him, and Covington laughed as he took a sip of his drink.

"I did."

"Ladies don't drink brandy," Eric said, furrowing his brow, and it was Ashford who answered him.

"These ones do."

Before Eric had a chance to ask any further questions, Ashford started in on the one topic that had captured his focus for nearly the past year.

His treasure hunt.

"Are you ready for your journey, Ferrington?"

"I am," Eric answered. "Everything at home is looked after and I have brought with me all that I shall require. I am to set sail within the week."

"Perfecto," Ashford said with a small smile. *"Gracias."*

"De nada," Eric said, in reference to the fact that out of all of them, he spoke Spanish the most fluently, making him the most suitable of them all to attempt to solve this clue. "I am intrigued as to just what could be awaiting me."

"I am as well," Ashford said, shaking his head as he leaned

THE LORD'S COMPASS

back. "First we had the riddle that Cassandra and Covington deduced here at Castleton which led us to the code that Whitehall and Lady Hope had to solve with the books. That of course led us to the necklace which your brother and Lady Percy tracked down in Bath. I just wish the scrap of paper they found within it gave us more information than simply the name of a city in Spain."

"It's not much, but I have confidence it will all work out," Eric said, clapping a hand on his friend's shoulder.

"Eric?"

"It is the bridegroom himself!" Eric said, turning at the voice before reaching his arm out across his brother's shoulders and pulling him in closer toward him. "How is married life?"

"So far, very similar to unmarried life, but that is sure to change soon," Noah said, adjusting his glasses. "Eric, can I speak to you?"

"Why so serious?" Eric asked, reading the expression on his brother's face. "Today is a day of celebration."

Noah looked around at the rest of them and sighed, apparently deciding that his only option was to share with all of them what was on his mind. He was always far too worried about the future. Eric wished he would enjoy the moment – especially on a day like today.

"I have been thinking about this trip of yours to Spain."

"You are going to miss me, are you not?" Eric said jokingly, even though deep within he knew it was the truth. He and Noah might be as different as could be, but he would miss his brother – and he knew the feeling would be reciprocated.

"Yes, but that is not my concern," Noah said. "I am not sure if now is the best time to be travelling to Spain. I know we are not currently in conflict with the country, but the waters are somewhat perilous for an English ship due to our skirmishes with the French. In Spain, if you are discovered—"

"Noah," Eric stopped him, holding his palm up. "That is the beauty of this. I am not going to be an Englishman when I go there."

"What do you mean?"

"The very reason I volunteered for this is because I can speak Spanish – and I can speak it rather well," he said, unconcerned about modesty when it was the truth. "I am going to pretend I am a Spaniard."

"That is all very well, but what if the truth is discovered?"

"What is the worst that could happen? They would not want to cause an issue with their new allies by untoward action against an English nobleman," Eric answered with a shrug, although the concern had reared itself within him.

"Well—"

"Ferrington, you do know that you do not have to go?" Ashford cut in. "I appreciate what you have offered to do for me, truly I do, but perhaps your brother has a point. Discovering the next clue in this treasure hunt is not worth your life."

Eric waved them away. "My life? You are all being overly dramatic. I will be just fine. I have it all figured out."

He planned to take things one day at a time and see what happened, but he wasn't about to tell them that, for he knew most of them would far prefer he had an idea of what he was going to do once he arrived.

"Very well. But if anything changes, do not hesitate to return, even without the treasure or the next clue," Ashford said, and Eric nodded.

"Of course."

"Now, shall we toast to the groom?" Eric asked, summoning a footman to bring them another drink. When they were all prepared, he lifted his glass. "To love."

"To love," they echoed before clinking their glasses together. Eric's spilled slightly, for he was suddenly no longer focused on what he was doing.

No, his gaze was across the room – arrested by the woman staring back at him. But it wasn't affection in her eyes.

No. It was undisguised disdain.

And it was all for him.

* * *

"Faith?"

Percy approached, looking as beautiful as she ever had, her pale blue dress the perfect accent to her long auburn curls.

"Percy. You are radiant."

"Thank you," she replied with a smile. "That is happiness."

"Well, I am happy *for* you," Faith said, taking Percy's hands as her sister joined them. "I am happy for both of you. You have found the men who complete you."

"You will one day," Hope said in that optimistic way of hers.

Faith inwardly rolled her eyes but pretended all was fine. She would not be a cynic today of all days. She would smile and say what they wanted from her.

"Perhaps."

That was as good as she could do. She couldn't bring herself to tell them how wrong they were, that she would never marry, would never find a man she preferred.

"I know what you are thinking," Hope said, reading right through her façade. "But it will happen. I am certain of it."

Faith just nodded.

"That was why I came over here," Percy said. "You seem rather… glum."

"Not at all," Faith said, shaking her head. "I was simply observing the room. Nothing of which to be concerned."

"Where did you go?" Hope asked.

"When?"

"A while ago," Cassandra said as she joined them with her hands around her growing stomach, evidently having overheard the last bit of their conversation. She had insisted on attending the wedding, even though she expected the baby to come in just a couple of months. After this, she had promised her husband, Lord Covington, they would return home and stay there until well after the baby's arrival. "You were gone for nearly an hour."

"I was outside," she said, not wanting to get into details.

"You needed time alone," Hope said understandingly, always aware of what her sister required.

"I did."

"But Lord Ferrington found you, didn't he?" Percy asked with a small smile.

"Why would you think that?"

"I saw him enter the room slightly before you and he had that look on his face – the one which is a rather confusing mix of desperation, humor, and exasperation. He always wears it after a conversation with you."

Faith's mouth dropped open as Madeline walked up to them, completing their quintet.

"That cannot be true... can it?" she asked, and Madeline looked around at all of them.

"What are we talking about?" she asked.

"About how Faith drives Lord Ferrington mad when she rebukes his affections."

"Ah yes," Madeline agreed. "That you do. I do not know why he continues to want you so when you speak to him as you do."

THE LORD'S COMPASS

"He does not want me," Faith muttered, disgruntled. "He only continues to needle me because I am the one woman who does not fall for his charms. I am not that rude to him... am I?"

Hope gave her a knowing look, fully aware of what happened between Faith and Lord Ferrington in the past, but Faith chose to ignore her. When she turned away it was only to capture Percy's pitying gaze.

"What do we think of entrusting him with this journey to San Sebastian?" Faith asked instead.

"He seems up for the adventure, despite the political atmosphere," Cassandra said with a shrug. "The rest of us have all solved clues in this treasure hunt. I suppose he can do the same."

"But what is he supposed to do with a clue that is simply a piece of paper upon which is written the name of a city?" Faith asked, holding her hands out. "That is not much to go on."

"You are right, it's not," Cassandra said slowly. "But as this all seems to be connected to our family, perhaps there will be clues in Spain near our family's estate or from the necklace or the key. It all has to lead somewhere."

"I am just not sure if he should go alone."

"And just who should go with him?" Madeline asked, a twinkle in her eye, and Faith rolled her eyes and looked away from her.

"One of the men."

"None of the others can leave at the moment," Hope said gently. "He will be fine, Faith. There is nothing to worry about."

"I am not worried about *him*," she countered. "I am worried that he will stall this treasure hunt before we can finish it."

"I do not think you give him enough credit," Cassandra

said. "Lord Ferrington enjoys his fun, true, but he does look after an entire earldom."

"Everyone knows his mother does everything," Faith countered. "She has since his father passed."

"Well, he was rather young at the time," Hope said, and Faith had to bite her tongue. Hope had been the eternal optimist ever since they were children – although Faith wondered how much of it was to balance her own realism.

"He's not a young man anymore. He has to learn to settle down," she said, looking over at him, catching him staring at her once more.

"All will be fine," Madeline said, patting her hand. "Nothing to worry about. Now, Hope, I hear that you and Lord Whitehall are finally getting away together."

Hope launched into details of their travel plans – plans that would take Hope further from her – but Faith couldn't leave her concerns behind.

As Hope spoke, however, an idea began to form in Faith's mind. It was ludicrous, she knew. But it just might work.

CHAPTER 3

The smile on Eric's face grew wider the longer he stood at the bow of the ship and stared out over the water. He was aboard a packet ship, one on which, hopefully, he would not capture too much attention. He was to be a merchant returning to Spain, visiting San Sebastian to pick up some textiles. There were only six other cabins on board, and, upon boarding, most of the other passengers seemed uninterested in him.

The crew was also minimal, and Eric had paid dearly for his small, private cabin. No one else could discover that he was, in fact, an English earl. The captain was aware but he had agreed – for another fee – to keep his secret.

They had set sail earlier that day, and Eric was already enjoying the freedom the ocean provided, the spray of the saltwater, and the freshness of life that awaited him.

So different from the stale, stodgy air at home that smelled of responsibility and staidness.

He enjoyed his life. He was able to do as he pleased, to come and go according to his whims. He had funds enough to spend without worry. He didn't have to toil his days away, giving all of himself to simply afford the necessities of life. But sometimes – just sometimes – he wondered what it would have been like to be born into a different life. One with more choice. A second son, perhaps.

But there was no use in wondering, for it didn't make much difference, now did it?

After his conversation with Faith at Castleton, he had hoped to find her again, to have a chance to explain himself and what had happened. But she had obviously made certain she would not be caught alone with him again. Every time he saw her, she was with her sister or one of her friends. She had left Castleton shortly after the wedding and he finally resigned himself to the fact that she was never going to forgive him and, most likely, he would never have a chance to speak to her again.

It made him angrier than anything ever had in some time.

"How long until we arrive?" he called up to the captain, who was standing at the helm, his hands on the wheel.

"Depends."

"On?"

"The wind, mostly. That will affect our speed. And it will take some extra time keeping our distance from the coast of France."

"So…"

"A week or two."

"Thank you," Eric said.

"You in a hurry?" the captain asked, the pipe between his teeth bobbing up and down as he spoke, encouraging Eric to fish through his own pocket for his cheroot.

"No, actually," Eric said. "I have all the time in the world."

He wandered down the few stairs and back to the bow, gazing out over the sea. It was calm here. Soothing. He loved his clubs and enjoyed all that London and the cities had to offer him, but they also made him appreciate these moments

THE LORD'S COMPASS

of peace between. Not that he would ever admit that to anyone.

Eric couldn't have said how long he stood there, watching the coast as they travelled alongside it, but when darkness fell, his stomach began to rumble and he realized that he hadn't eaten in hours and dinner was likely being served. He swayed with the gentle rocking motions of the ship downward, arriving in time for a quick meal, as most of the other passengers had already finished, before he pushed open the door of the small, sparse cabin. He was emptying his pockets when he stopped, suddenly aware that something was amiss. He wasn't alone.

He turned around slowly, wondering if one of the crew had decided to rob him. Would they throw him overboard? He had brought his pistols with him, but he hadn't worn them. Foolish. From now on he would—but if they killed him now, there wouldn't *be* a future.

He no longer had any time to wonder what could happen, however, as his slow turn around finally stopped and his gaze was arrested on the bed before him – and the woman sitting upon it.

He blinked a few times, certain that he must have been drugged. For this couldn't be real – could it? There was no chance that Lady Faith Embury was primly seated on his bed awaiting him. That would be a dream. Mayhap he had already fallen asleep.

But then she spoke, and while her voice haunted his dreams on a usual night, in his imaginings, she was lovely, kind, and had only words of endearment for him. Which was how he knew that this was reality, for what came out of her mouth was as ornery as ever

"Lord Ferrington. It took you long enough."

* * *

THE LOOK on his face nearly convinced her that this had all been worth it.

She had questioned herself from the moment she had boarded the ship. Through her uneasiness unpacking in her cabin, while picking the lock on his door, over the hours she had waited for him to arrive, and most especially when he had stepped into his cabin.

She had – unfairly, she knew – grown rather annoyed with him for taking so long. As far as she knew, this was his cabin, so why hadn't he arrived sooner? She had paced fitfully for hours and now that he had finally entered, unwelcome relief had swept over her.

His presence should not make her feel so... safe. Relieved. Home.

Faith had to fight the urge to stand and run into his arms in gratefulness at seeing him. Which bothered her more than she cared to admit.

"What in the hell are you doing here?" he asked, more shocked than angry as his mouth gaped open.

His reaction worked to quell any of her unexpected longings for him.

He was so tall, so broad that he seemed to fill the entirety of the small cabin.

"I am here to help," she said, squaring her shoulders as she stood and walked the few steps toward him. "I didn't think you should search for this clue or treasure or whatever it may be alone."

"So you thought that *you* would assist me?" He looked around the room as though searching for something. "Who has accompanied you?"

"No one. I am here alone."

"Unchaperoned on this ship."

"Do you think I would be here in your cabin if I had a chaperone escorting me?"

THE LORD'S COMPASS

"You are an unmarried young lady. The fact that you are alone with me here in my cabin—"

He was running his hands through his silky, long dark hair now, obviously disconcerted. She had never quite seen him like this and she had to say she was rather enjoying this part of her reveal.

"Not to worry," she said brusquely, rubbing her hands together. "I have my cabin. And I have a plan in place."

"A plan..." he murmured, his fingers now on his temples. "How did you board the ship without my notice? How long have you been in my cabin? Have you eaten anything?"

She was not affected by his multiple questions and, in fact, answered them quite succinctly.

"I boarded when you were speaking with the captain," she said, not admitting that she had waited until he wasn't looking so that he couldn't prevent her from boarding. "I ensured that no one noticed me. It was earlier this morning, shortly after you had stowed your items in your cabin. I haven't yet eaten but said I would do so in private."

"So what *is* your plan, then? You are just going to sail with me to Spain and hope that your parents do not notice that you are not currently residing in their home?"

"The timing worked out rather perfectly, actually," she said, pleased with herself and hoping that he would also note her ingenuity. "Hope and Lord Whitehall were leaving at nearly the same time for their journey up to the Highlands. I told my parents that I was going with them."

"They did not think it was odd you would want to accompany a newly married couple?"

"I told them that since I have no plans on marrying, this would likely be my only opportunity for such travel. I told them that I planned to give Hope and Lord Whitehall time alone, but that I would be their travel companion. My parents were quite agreeable. I believe they hoped that I might find myself a husband on the way. It seems that they are desperate enough to be rid of me that they do not mind if I am lost to a Highlander."

She attempted to smile, even though the thought pained her. It seemed that her parents were all too eager to give her away, ignoring the fact that she had a plan for her life that did not involve a husband.

"Did you tell Hope?" he asked, sitting in the chair before the desk, seeming more interested than shocked now, finally accepting that this was happening.

"I will write to her and tell her shortly. She has no reason to not help me in this, however, as she did nearly the same thing not so long ago. I had the carriage take me to the harbour, where my parents thought I would be meeting up with her and Whitehall. Instead, I used the money my father provided me to purchase a berth on this ship to Bilibio, the closest port to San Sebastian."

"I see," he said, the only sound in the room now the tapping of his boot against the floor. "Do you have a lock on your door?"

"I assume so," she said, taken aback at the question. "Why do you ask?"

He looked at her incredulously. "Lady Faith, you are many things, but stupid you are not."

"I hardly think that any of the other passengers and, most especially the crew, would risk the repercussions of taking advantage of a lady."

He was already shaking his head, and she couldn't help but note how their roles had reversed. Usually, he was the one thinking the best of people, but it seemed that in this, he had seen the worst.

"When men are at sea without the opportunity for female companionship, they often become desperate – especially when they are in their cups. We shall have to create a story on who you are to me. At least it appears you have brought some Spanish attire."

"I have and I have also thought of my role," she said swiftly. "I will proclaim myself to be your widowed sister."

He snorted. "That will never work."

"Whyever not?" she asked. Surely she was good enough to be considered a familial relation.

"It just won't," he said stiffly, looking away from her.

"Your cousin, then?"

"No."

"You must give me a reason why you do not think that will suffice."

"Because…" he scratched his chin. "Because I cannot help the way that I look at you, and the sailors will likely notice."

"The way that you look at me?"

"Yes," he said, punching a hand out in the air, as though he wasn't pleased about having to tell her this. "Like… a woman. A woman who I… appreciate."

"Oh," she said, taken aback by his words. He had always teasingly chased after her, but she thought that it was more so because she was the one woman who no longer readily gave into his charms. Not because he had any particular appreciation for her.

"Are you sure you mean me?" she asked mockingly. "Most men are too captivated by Hope to see past her toward me."

"Yes," he said, turning the full bore of his gaze upon her now. "I most certainly mean you, Faith."

Her lips parted as she seemed to lose all of her breath, caught in the intensity of his eyes, the hazel irises rimmed in such thick black.

"I-I had no idea that you thought such a thing." Not anymore, at least. He had made it clear she was nothing special to him.

"I am sure I made that abundantly clear," he said. "I am

not a man who hides his emotions. I showed you that night how much you meant to me."

"I am not the only woman that you kiss," she scoffed.

"Did I not show you afterward, when I gave you so much of my attention?"

"I always assumed you were toying with me. You are a man of many jests, after all."

"That may be true," he acknowledged. "But when it comes to you, Faith, I never jest."

They paused, the air tense between them, before he asked the questions she wished he hadn't. "Why did you come? Why risk everything?"

Faith tried to hide the guilt on her face, but she knew the moment he realized exactly why. "You do not trust me," he said, his eyes widening and his mouth falling open. "You do not think I can do this."

"It's not that," she said hastily. "It is just that I think anyone could use help with this task and—"

"I am not as incompetent as you think, Faith," he said, his jaw tightening, showing a rare moment of displeasure, causing a twinge in her belly.

"I never said that. I—"

"I should go find the captain. I need to inquire about the other passengers," he said, turning on his heel, and, before she could say another word, he left, slamming the door behind him.

CHAPTER 4

Not much ever caught Eric off guard, but Faith had knocked him off any equilibrium he had found on this ship. He was pleased to see her, yes, more so than he should have been, but if he didn't know better, he would wonder if this woman was, in fact, the Faith he knew. That practical woman seemed to have disappeared, leaving in her place a reckless woman who took risks that could have consequences which would forever change both of their lives. If there was any woman he must be compromised with, he was glad it was Faith – but he would have preferred any promise they made to one another was her choice and not like this.

He would have thought that he would like this side of her – it was, after all, how he typically lived his life. Impulsively. Recklessly. In such opposition to her orderly straightforwardness. Which was why he was surprised at how disconcerted he was by her appearance on this ship.

And then there was the fact that the only reason she was here was because she had no faith in him. He kicked a pile of rope as he walked by it, but it was so heavy that he did nothing but bruise his toe and earn himself a glare from one of the crew members.

He was also annoyed that she was putting herself at such risk. It was one thing for him to travel to Spain and disguise himself as a local. How was she going to do so? Clothing was one thing, but he doubted she even spoke a word of Spanish.

He sighed, lighting a cheroot as he stopped to look around, finding only a few crew members about as the sun began to set, casting a beautiful orange glow over the horizon, warming his face and settling him somewhat.

"Thought you were going for a bite," the captain said, startling him, but of course he was present, steering them along the English coast.

"I am," Eric replied. "I returned for the sunset."

"Seen many in my time," the captain said slowly, wistfulness in his voice. "Never gets old."

"I do not suppose it does," Eric agreed. "Say, how many cabins did you say were aboard this ship?"

"Six for passengers," the captain replied.

"Right," Eric said with a nod.

"Yours not good enough?" The captain asked, obviously prepared to defend his ship.

"All is well," Eric said hastily, not wanting to start a row with the man he was currently trusting to safely transport him to Spain with a secret. "Perfectly well. Fine. Perfectly fine, that is."

"I can send a crew member in to—"

"No, no," Eric said, waving a hand at him. "No, no, no."

The captain lifted a brow, and Eric hoped that he would believe his erratic behaviour was simply that of an eccentric aristocrat who was not used to such sparse surroundings.

"Who are the other passengers aboard?" he asked.

"Well, there is a woman..." the captain began with a knowing look at Eric, but he quickly quelled his suspicion by raising a hand in the air.

"Yes," Eric said. "She is travelling with me."

"Is she now," the captain said, obviously interested, but Eric didn't explain further.

"Yes," he said, clearing his throat, feeling guilty about lying to the captain. "Are there any other passengers who might be a... threat to her?"

"Shouldn't be," the captain said with a shrug. "One family, a pair of women, and the rest are men but seem to be good sorts."

"And the crew?"

The captain bristled. "I chose them myself. They're a fine lot of men."

"Apologies. I mean no insult. Goodnight, Captain," Eric finally said, unable to think of anything else to say that might improve the situation or provide him with more information.

"Goodnight, my lord."

Eric stopped in front of his cabin door, took a deep breath of sustenance, and then pushed through the door, back to either heaven or hell. He wasn't yet certain which to call it.

* * *

"I've been thinking—" Faith began when Eric walked into the room, only she spoke at the same time as he did. "Pardon me?"

"You need to get off this ship."

"Why?" she asked, affronted. Here she thought he enjoyed her company.

"Because there are many men on this ship and you are alone. Unchaperoned. It cannot be safe."

"I believe I can be the judge of that myself, but thank you for your concern," she said, her nostrils flaring, and he lifted his hands in exasperation.

"You do not understand the desperation of some men, Faith! And besides that, I am trying to evade notice. How can I do so if you are accompanying me about the ship?"

"I am not a woman many men notice. It is not as though Hope is here."

"*I* notice you. They will too."

"What are you thinking?" she asked dully, ignoring him.

"We are travelling along the English coast," Eric said. "When we reach Plymouth, you can disembark."

"And go where?" she asked incredulously. "My home is across the country!"

"I do not know," he said with a shrug. "You found your way here. You should be able to follow that path back home again."

"You cannot be serious. I would be alone," she said, aghast.

"You are alone here," he countered.

"No, I am not," she said. "I am with you."

The words were off her tongue before she knew what she was saying, and her mouth snapped shut as she realized what she had said.

It took a moment for him to register them, and then his eyes brightened, widening as he stared down at her.

"I make you feel safe?" he asked with joy in his eyes.

"I never said safe," she retorted, crossing her arms and looking around the room, stepping toward the shelf to look at the books that lined it. They were not, however, books, she realized as she peered at them. They were maps.

THE LORD'S COMPASS

"You said you were not alone because you were with me."

"Yes." She looked back at him. "Which is the case. I am here, standing in this room with you. When I return to my cabin, you will still be aboard the ship."

He nodded, although he didn't appear to be giving up on his interpretation of her words, even though she had only meant it as she had said.

"Needless to say, you want to be with me, as you are here," he said, and she could only roll her eyes. "But that cannot be."

That had her snapping her head up to look at him. As far as she knew, ever since she had turned cold toward him, he had been in pursuit of her. What had changed? Had he thought that he had caught her – that he had *won*?

Not that this was a game.

"Tell me, Lord Ferrington, just why you would feel that way."

"Because this is not a safe place for you. Ships sink, Faith. All the time. Especially during wartime."

"England is not at war."

He snorted. "We are only between wars. That is what peacetime is."

"How very pessimistic of you, Lord Ferrington," she couldn't help but point out. It seemed the man who thought in rainbows and sunshine had a dark side after all.

"My father was an officer in the army," he said. "I know war all too well."

"Would you ever fight, yourself?"

"Not if I can help it," he said.

"How very honest of you."

He shrugged. "That is how it is, Faith. Like it or not. Killing other men is not in my nature."

"Well," she said, smoothing her hands over her skirts, "now that you know I am here and am available to help you once we reach Spain, I shall return to my cabin. I requested to have dinner awaiting me and I have grown quite hungry."

"Faith, I still think you should stay in England. I am posing as a Spaniard. As an Englishwoman, how are you going to—"

"Que pases una buena noche, amigo mío. Hasta mañana," she said, bidding him goodnight and a promise to see him tomorrow as she made for the door. She desperately wanted to turn around to see his reaction, but she couldn't – for to do so would only allow him to see the smile on her face.

* * *

ERIC HAD SMILED to himself when he had heard Faith's cabin door shut soundly a few seconds after her exit. So she was right next door to him. Good. He would, at least, be able to keep an eye on her – not that he would ever tell her that, for he knew exactly what she would say to his belief that he needed to take care of her.

She could take care of herself. He could practically hear her saying it.

He could even hear her saying it in Spanish.

He snorted. He knew she had been proud of herself for surprising him like that. It made sense, though. She was an intelligent woman from a well-to-do family who would have had the best of governesses. She likely knew a great many languages.

Now he just had to figure out how the two of them would explain themselves once they arrived in San Sebastian.

A few hours later, he was lying in his hard, narrow bed, trying to fall asleep, although it was proving rather futile.

And it wasn't the fault of the bed. Or the ship. It was her, and the fact she was sleeping on just the other side of the thin ship wall.

He heard a thump and he wondered if she was also having trouble sleeping. Although she was so stoic, it was hard to believe that anything ever bothered her.

A slow creak suddenly resounded. Was that her door swinging open? But where could she possibly be going? He hoped she didn't think that she could take a midnight stroll alone on a ship. There was being a strong woman who could take care of herself and then there was simply being foolish.

He heard the tread of a boot on the floor – and then another. Slow, careful footsteps. But wait – that didn't make sense. If she had let herself out of the room, then the footsteps should be in the common area beyond the room and not coming from beyond the thin wall.

He pushed himself upright. Was she walking around herself – or was someone else in her room?

Should he go check, or was he being presumptuous?

Then it all happened so quickly – a shout, a grunt, a thud – that Eric was out of bed and in the corridor before he had even determined just what he was going to do.

He pushed through the unlocked door into the cabin that was even smaller than his, with hardly any room to even walk around the wardrobe and small bed. Two figures were on the bed itself, attached in a violent embrace. Faith was doing an admirable job of defending herself, limbs flailing as she held nothing back, kicking, scratching, punching – but her attacker was much larger than she was, and a mix of panic and fury rose within Eric like a gushing geyser.

"Get your hands off of her!" he shouted, uncaring that others may hear him – in fact, he hoped they did.

His shout was enough to surprise the man, who obviously hadn't heard him coming, as he reared up, providing Faith with the opportunity to escape. But Faith being Faith, instead of jumping off the bed and running out of his clasp, she reared back her hand and brought her fist forward, connecting with her attacker's nose. There was a satisfying crunch as his head snapped back. From his cry, Eric wondered if she had broken his nose.

He reached out, wrenching the man off of her, throwing him onto the floor beside them. Eric was strong, but he surprised even himself at the surge of power that had emerged when seeing Faith so threatened.

She jumped off the bed, stumbling slightly when she hit the floor before falling forward into Eric's arms. He'd like to think that she was seeking refuge with him but he was well aware that the more likely truth was that there was simply nowhere else for her to land in the small space.

Eric was torn between chasing the man himself and keeping hold of Faith. He placed his hands on her shoulders, preparing to set her back so that he could go after the bastard who had dared to come for her when she suddenly reached out and clutched his upper right arm with her left hand.

"Eric?"

Her voice was softer now – he would have said weaker, but he knew better.

"You're all right now," he said, doing his best to reassure her. "I'm here. I've got you."

"I think I broke my hand."

He reached down, quickly at first, toward her other flailing hand but gentled when he saw her flinch. He cupped her hand within his, her bare skin nearly scorching him, but his reaction was inconsequential to whatever pain she was feeling.

As he inspected her hand, motion came from behind him and he spun around as the man began to rise. Eric crossed toward him in two steps, lifting him and wrenching his arm behind him.

"You yellow-bellied—"

"What is going on in here?"

They turned toward the door, which was now filled with a couple of the crew members and the captain.

"The lady was attacked," Eric practically growled. "By this man."

He pushed the man toward him, and the captain held up his torch, casting light onto the attacker's face.

"Who are you?" Eric asked.

"Another passenger," the captain said once he had a better look. "Mr. Smith, isn't it?"

"Wasn't doing anything," the man growled. "Just a mistake. Thought this was my cabin."

Faith began to protest from behind them, but her annoyance was so half-hearted that Eric knew she was in pain.

"Could you bring me a bucket of seawater? Or something cold?" Eric asked, and a crewman nodded.

"Are you going to be all right, miss?" the other crewman asked.

"Yes," she said, with a small smile that Eric expected was supposed to be reassuring but instead appeared quite pained. "Thank you."

"Say, *Señor*," the captain said, staring at Eric. "what are you doing in here?"

"I heard the noise and the shout and came to see what was the matter."

The captain nodded, before looking suspiciously first at Eric and then Faith. "Leavin' her now?"

"No," he said, shaking his head. "She cannot be alone. Not after this. And she needs someone to look after her hand."

"Apologies, but can't leave another man alone in here with her even if you are acquaintances. Didn't bring a chaperone, miss?" the captain said. "Have to know things like this will happen if you don't."

Faith bristled beside Eric, and he put a hand down over

top of hers. He had no desire to draw further attention to either of them – or to have the captain questioning him or Faith.

"She doesn't need a companion, as she is safe with me," he said, setting his jaw. "For she is my wife."

CHAPTER 5

"Is this true?" The captain looked at Faith with doubt in his gaze. "You are his wife?"

Faith looked at Eric, who was staring at her with urgency in his eyes.

"Y-yes," she said, nodding, still trying to come to terms with all that had just happened to her while also managing the pain that was radiating from her hand. "I am his wife."

"Why are you in this cabin alone, then?" he asked, one bushy white eyebrow raised.

"Why do we not save that story for tomorrow?" Eric said, stepping forward, and for once, Faith was pleased with his ability to confront every person and situation with relative ease.

"Very well," the captain said, apparently tired enough that he didn't overly care about this situation any longer. "I hope you now understand that there are dangers on every ship. And that it is not my men to be concerned about."

"We understand," Eric said with a nod. "We do wonder what will happen to Mr. Smith here."

"Well," the captain said with a shrug. "He paid for a cabin

like everyone else. Nothing actually happened to your... wife, now did it? It was Mr. Smith who came away from the exchange injured. So I suppose it was as he said – he had his cabins mixed up."

Faith stepped forward, ready to tell the captain exactly what she thought of his insinuation that she had practically invited the man to come attack her, but Eric placed a hand over her good one, gripping it tightly.

"Very well," he said, although his jaw was taut, as though he also didn't appreciate the captain's reaction. He nodded to the returning crew member who had retrieved a bucket of water for them. "Goodnight, Captain."

The captain ushered his crewmen and Mr. Smith out, the latter looking behind him with a lecherous grin that had Faith's skin crawling and her anger boiling.

When the door closed behind them, she turned to Eric, unable to contain herself for any longer.

"What was that about?" she hissed. "Not only did you allow the man to get away with attacking me, but the captain insulted me with no repercussion and you named me as your wife on top of it!"

He led her to the bed, lifting the bucket onto the small table beside them. She allowed him to guide her hand into it, closing her eyes at the relief the icy water provided, which overcame the sting of the salt water when it hit the small cuts on her knuckles.

"I am aware that the situation is less than ideal," he said, pacing back and forth, although the size of the room only allowed him two to three steps in either direction, which meant that Faith was becoming dizzy just watching him. "But the entire point of this journey is to make it surreptitiously. San Sebastian is not a big city. If we arrive with any scandal or question attached to our names, the locals will be distrustful, which is the exact opposite of what we want. We cannot have them knowing who we truly are."

"*We* do not even know who we are supposed to be at this point," she said with a sigh, and he nodded.

"You're right. Well, I've said we're married now—"

"Without consulting me."

"What was I supposed to do, Faith?" he said. "I hate to say it, but the captain has a point. The other passengers were aware that you were staying alone and unchaperoned. It was only a matter of time until something happened. Which is unfortunate, but it's the way it is. And, as it happens, a married couple will attract far less attention than a single woman."

She snorted, looking away. She hated that he was right. She hated that this was the way of it.

"At least now, I have a reason for keeping an eye on you, for ensuring that you are safe," he continued.

"And just how are you going to do that?" she asked.

"You will come and stay in my cabin."

Her mouth dropped open.

"Absolutely not."

"There is no other option," he said, crossing his arms over his chest, his thin white nightshirt doing nothing to hide the straining strength of his arms and shoulders. "Besides, my cabin is bigger than yours."

"The size of the cabins is not the cause for my objection," she said wryly.

He ignored her, walking over to the wardrobe.

"What are you doing?" she asked indignantly.

"Packing your things," he said, finding her valise at the bottom and beginning to throw her dresses into it unceremoniously.

"Have you never packed before?" she asked nearly incredulously.

"Not really," he said without any shame. "Have a valet for that, usually."

"I shall do it myself," she said, and he shook his head.

"Not with that hand," he said. "Not tonight."

"Tomorrow, then."

"No. You will come to my room tonight."

"I will most certainly not."

The more he ignored her, the angrier she became. She knew, deep within that part of her that didn't want to admit the truth, even to herself, that she was mostly upset at the situation she had placed herself in that had led to all of this, and the lack of control she had over what came next.

But it was much easier to be angry with him – even if it seemed she had no choice but to do what he said.

She sat there, silently fuming as her hand froze itself to blessed numbness, as he prepared everything – including handling her undergarments, although he did not seem perturbed in the least. He'd likely seen plenty of those before. Finally, he looked around, pleased with himself.

"Well, that's it," he said. "I'll take this over and then return for you."

"I can walk myself," she said. "At least pass me my wrapper so I'm not walking the ship in my nightgown."

He nodded, apparently completely unaffected that they had remained together in such deshabille. Although her nightgown probably covered far more than he was used to seeing women wearing in their chambers in the middle of the night.

He helped her into the wrapper, taking particular care of her injured hand. He lifted her valise in one hand and went to take the bucket with the other, but she waved him off.

"I can lift it myself," she said.

"Very well," he said, as they began the slow but short walk to his cabin. "Do you truly think it is broken?"

"No," she said with a sigh at her overreaction, but it had certainly been painful. "Now that it's been a few minutes, I would guess that it's likely just bruised. Which is good. I would hate not being able to use it."

"How could you ever shoot that bow of yours?"

She knew he was joking, but his statement was truer than he realized. Others saw archery as a pastime, but for her, it allowed her to release so much of the emotion that she kept within herself.

She stopped in the doorway of his cabin. He had been correct that it was bigger than hers, but not by much.

"How are the two of us going to live here together?" she asked, her mouth dropping open. "There is but one small bed and no private space for me to change my clothing or—or—" she couldn't bring herself to say the rest.

"I am happy to turn my back or leave when required," he said. "As for sleeping, you can take the bed. I shall gather the blankets from your cabin and sleep on the floor."

"You cannot be serious."

"Very well," he said with a nonchalant shrug. "If you'd like to take the floor, that would be preferable for me."

"I am not sleeping on the floor."

"Share the bed, then?" he asked, one corner of his lips uplifted and his eyes twinkling.

Faith would have liked to tell him exactly what she thought of that suggestion, but she couldn't help the short laugh that emerged.

"Oh, she responds to some humor, then," he said.

She sat on the bed, holding her hand.

"I am not a complete witch."

"I never said you were."

She dropped her head, unable to look him in the eye. "I know that's what everyone thinks of me. That I am the ice queen. Devoid of emotion. Unsympathetic. Unloving. Unlovable."

"No one thinks that, Faith," he said, sitting down next to her, lifting her injured hand out of the bucket before placing the bucket of water on the floor and lifting her arm by the wrist, taking a closer look at her injury.

"I have to ask you something," she said, her heart pounding a bit harder, although whether it was from his touch or the conversation, she wasn't entirely sure.

"Yes?"

"You always say that you want me, that you lust after me."

"Yes, I do," he said, unapologetically.

"Do you mean it? Or is it some kind of joke?"

She looked him square in the eye, then, needing him to understand how serious she was in her question, prepared to determine if his answer was true or not.

"Why would you ask me that?"

"Because I can hardly see why you would unless it is all some kind of game to you. Or is it simply because I am the one woman who tells you no?"

He leaned in toward her, lifting a hand and cradling her face within it. Faith hated herself for pressing her cheek closer to him.

"It's not a joke, Faith. I mean it."

"But why?"

He shrugged. "Hell if I know. It'd be easier if I didn't."

"Although there are not many women you wouldn't be interested in, now, are there?"

He dropped his hand. "Is that what you think of me?"

"It's the truth, isn't it?"

He turned his head away, and an unwelcome ache bloomed in Faith's chest. Why did she need him to want her – and only her – so badly? She had tried to avoid the man for the past few years, had done all she could to turn him off of her. But the more she did so, the harder he came. The thrill of the chase, she supposed.

"Go to bed, Faith," was all he said, and she wondered if she had hurt his feelings.

"But—"

He turned to her, his face in shadow. "You need your sleep. Your hand does look like it will be fine once the cuts and bruises heal. But are you otherwise all right after that attack? He didn't… hurt you in any other way?"

"He didn't," she said softly. "You came in time." She paused. "Thank you for that. For coming. If you hadn't—" her voice hitched, and his response was like a warm caress.

"Do not think of it, Faith. I was there. That's all that matters."

As he created his bed on the floor, she lay back onto his blankets, his musky scent from where he had been sleeping but a short time before surrounding her.

Eric Rowley was showing her a different side to himself. A side that interested her. And she didn't like it.

Not one bit.

CHAPTER 6

"Owww," Eric couldn't help but groan as he awoke that morning on the hard floorboards. He pushed himself into a sitting position despite the protest from his muscles.

He looked over to the bed to see if he had bothered Faith, but she was still sleeping soundly. Her head was facing to the side of the room, strands of her dark blond hair having emerged from her plait and draped over his pillow.

She seemed so peaceful in her slumber, and Eric couldn't help but rest back on his heels and watch her for a few minutes, enjoying this view of her.

Her opinion of him last night had hurt a little, but mostly because there was more truth to it than he would care to admit. He did like to have fun, and he had never seen the harm in enjoying a fair bit of spirits and a fair number of women. Two years ago, he had been prepared to give himself to Faith and only Faith, but she had made it clear that she wasn't interested in him, and so he had moved on as best he could.

She was right, to an extent. Part of the reason that he had

continued to pursue her was *because* she resisted all of his efforts. But it wasn't because he enjoyed the chase. It was because he never understood why she had spurned him so after initially showing interest and it had eaten away at him. When she began to get to know him —the real him – had she not liked what she saw? Or was it truly because of this kiss she supposedly witnessed?

Would he stop flirting with the other women if he had her? Perhaps. But perhaps it was too late for that.

For now, he had to focus on getting them both through this journey with their lives and their reputations intact. Then he would worry about what came next.

Faith began to murmur, and he leaned over, settling his weight on the bed next to her.

"Faith?"

"Eric?" she said, her eyes blinking open sleepily. "What are you—oh!"

She pushed herself up into a sitting position as she looked around the small room.

"You forgot where you were?"

"Yes," she said, looking up at him, and he had to admit that he liked seeing her like this, all dishevelled and far from the perfect princess she was always so concerned with portraying. "How was the floor?"

"Fine," he lied. He didn't want to give her any further reason to think that she had to return to her room. "How did you sleep?"

"Quite well, actually," she said. "Especially considering all that occurred last night."

"Must be because you knew that you had a handsome knight by your side."

"Must be," she said, although she frowned and Eric realized the levity of earlier was gone, as she had redonned her usual armour. "I'd like to dress for the day before we break our fast if you don't mind."

"Of course," he said. "I shall go next door to your former room until you are ready."

"But you are not prepared for the day yourself."

"Not yet," he said, before walking over to the wardrobe, opening it and finding his shirt and breeches within. With his back to Faith, he stripped his nightshirt over his head, leaving himself bare to her, before he began to dress himself, unable to keep from looking over his shoulder to see her reaction.

She was still sitting in bed, the linen bunched around her waist, but her mouth was open wide, gaping at him.

"What are you doing?" she finally managed.

"Dressing."

"But—I am right here!"

"It doesn't bother me."

"But it bothers *me*!"

"Turn around then," he said, before bending over to pick up his breeches, knowing he flashed her a look at his bottom, which, if he did say so himself, was quite well-defined and known to be an asset with women.

She let out an "eep" before diving under the blankets, and he couldn't help but chuckle.

"It's fine to like what you see!" he called out, and her only response was a muffled, "I cannot see anything!" from beneath the covers.

Aware that she would not be re-emerging, he dressed quickly, as best he could without his valet. It had been some time since he had done so, but he knew that having an English valet accompanying him would be of no help to the guise he was attempting to portray.

"You can come out now," he called, and Faith held the blanket up to cover her face except for peeking out with one eye as though distrustful of him before she fully uncovered herself. "How will you dress without a lady's maid?" he asked.

"I found dresses with larger fastenings," she said. "I will be able to dress myself."

"Well, I'm happy to help," he said, but she was shaking her head before he even finished his offer.

"I shall be fine," she said, and he shrugged before doing as she wished and leaving the room. He stood outside the door, nodding to the few passengers who strode by, watching for this Mr. Smith. He hadn't yet decided what he would do when he faced the man again. He may have let it go last night and would not be doing anything in view of the other passengers, but he would make it quite clear to the man that a threat toward Faith would not be tolerated – and now, as her "husband," he had a very valid reason for doing so.

He heard her call out, "Come in," and he re-entered the room, finding her standing there with her hands on her hips, a frown on her face, and her dress gaping open at the back.

"Do you require some assistance?" he asked, closing the door behind him and leaning one hip against the wall as he smirked at her.

She glared at him. "No need to gloat."

"I am not gloating."

"You are."

"Fine, maybe I am gloating a slight bit."

She sighed and turned around, causing Eric's smirk to quickly fade when presented with her bare back. Yes, part of it was covered with her chemise and clumsily tied stays, but her pale skin above the undergarments was still calling to him, all soft, silky cream.

"Eric?" she said, looking behind her, and he swallowed his desire and stepped toward her.

"Would you like me to retie your stays?" he asked, hearing the huskiness in his voice.

"Proficient in that, are you?" she said, but even through her biting remark, he could hear the breathiness of her voice and knew that she was as affected as he was.

"It is your choice," was all he said instead, and she nodded her head stiffly.

He reached out, sliding the silk ties from the bow she had – admirably if he was being honest – created behind her back, before carefully slightly tightening and then retying it.

He moved upward then, sliding each button through its hole, not preventing his fingers from brushing against her skin, and he caught her slight tremble with each touch. He stepped closer, tilting his head next to her neck, his mouth but an inch away as he longed to lean in and place his lips upon her. Her breathing quickened, and her fingers laced together in front of her. She wanted him as badly as he did her.

The only difference was that he knew, deep within, that she wasn't yet ready to admit it.

So he stepped back and away from her, clearing his throat, and she whirled around, the flush in her cheeks evident.

"Th-thank you," she said, and he nodded.

"Shall we go eat?"

"Why not?" she said, and they continued together out the door to the common area where the long table was set with food. They took a seat with the other passengers who had similarly purchased cabins.

"Good morning," Eric said, adding a slight touch of a Spanish accent to his English. They wanted everyone to believe they were Spanish, did they not? Still, he didn't miss Faith's sharp look, and he realized he should have explained more to her. He leaned in, not missing the opportunity to nuzzle his nose into her hair. "We are a married Spanish couple, do not forget."

She nodded slightly, a forced smile coming to her face as she sat next to him on the long bench, struggling to climb over it with her long skirts. Eric reached out and helped her lift them over.

Two men sat across from them, a couple around their age beside them next to Faith.

"It is lovely to see another woman aboard," the woman said, and Faith nodded, her gaze down on the food in front of her. "I am Patricia. Where are you from?"

"San—" Faith began, but Eric cut her words off.

"Barcelona."

"I see," the woman said, blinking in confusion. "You are Spanish, then."

"We are from Barcelona but visiting San Sebastian," he continued. "My wife was confused as she does not speak English well."

"My apologies," the woman said, although instead of slowing her speech as would likely help someone who struggled with a language, instead she simply raised her voice. "I wish I could speak Spanish to you in turn. I tried to learn, but never had the time."

"No matter," Faith said, and Eric nearly choked when she spoke, for her attempted Spanish accent was so far from what a true Spanish accent should be that it was near comical, but it didn't seem that the woman had any idea what it should sound like. "My English is not as bad as my husband believes."

"Good for you," the woman said. "We are going to visit my sister, who married an officer and then decided to stay in Spain. Haven't seen her since the wars finished."

"That will be lovely."

"And you?"

Faith looked over at Eric now, raising a brow in question, and he leaned in as a bowl of gruel was placed in front of him. He didn't look directly at Faith, for he knew that if he did, he would be unable to stop himself from laughing at her expression. From what he could see from the corner of his eye, she was not a fan of the dish.

"I am a merchant," he said. "I sell textiles. We are going to San Sebastian to trade."

"Interesting," the woman said, but before she could ask another question, one of the men from across the table leaned in.

"Say, wasn't the lady alone in a cabin?" he asked, chewing with his mouth open, and Eric had to stop his grimace.

"She was," he said, knowing that this was one truth they would be unable to hide. He wondered if Smith had been a friend of these men, for they seemed quite interested in Faith's travel circumstances.

"Heard you say you were married," the other man said. "If I had a wife like that—"

"Well, as it happens," Eric said, lifting the jug of ale in front of him and taking a big swig to give himself time to concoct a story, "my wife and I are newly reconciled."

That caught the attention of the couple next to them as well, as everyone leaned in to hear the gossip he was about to impart.

"We were separated, you see," he said dramatically. "Still married and working together, of course, but we were living different lives. My wife was unsure of me. Felt I was not the man she had believed I was."

He sighed, shaking his head, knowing his storytelling was over the top, but it seemed to be working – for now.

"But now?" Patricia asked breathlessly.

"Last night there was an incident," he said. "I was concerned for my wife, yes, to such an extent that I realized just how much I love her and what a fool I have been. I have asked her to reconcile with me, and she has, thank heavens, agreed." He reached for Faith's left hand and picked it up, bringing it to his lips and kissing it, looking her deeply in the eyes, surprised when he saw laughter there. "I am a lucky man."

"Oh, how romantic," Patricia said with a sigh. "You are both ever so fortunate."

"That I am," he said, winking at Faith. "That I am."

"So she is staying in your cabin?"

Eric turned back toward the men, dropping Faith's hand.

"You are awfully interested in my wife's whereabouts," he said, unable to help the ire in his tone. "Are you wondering for yourselves or your friend?"

"Our friend?" the one man said, although his lie – or omission – was far too obvious.

"Mr. Smith," Eric said, growling out the words.

"Don't know him," the one man said.

"Nope, not at all," the other lied, and Eric leaned in, lowering his voice so that just the two of them could hear him.

"Wherever he is hiding on this ship, perhaps you could give him a message for me."

"Very well."

"Stay away from my wife."

"Or else what?" the one man asked, lifting a brow. The two may not be noble, but they obviously had enough money to afford private cabins, which meant that they could, potentially, be a threat in the future.

"He does not want to discover 'what else.' Nor do you."

"Oh, we would never—"

"Unless the lady wanted it," the other man said, obviously cheekier than his friend.

"The lady does not want," Faith said through gritted teeth, and the man lifted both hands in front of him as though to ward off her ire.

"Understood," he said.

Eric turned toward her. "There is only one man who spends any time alone with you," he said, his arm brushing against hers and he reached by her for the teapot. "And that man is me."

CHAPTER 7

Despite Eric's commitment to do as Faith wished when it came time to change her clothes and do other business in the cabin, he couldn't leave every time for it would become far too suspicious.

And so, that night, Faith had to grit her teeth and trust that he wouldn't turn around while she was changing and using the wash basin to rinse herself. He hummed a tune as he faced the door, apparently completely unaffected by her actions.

When she was finished and securely covered in her nightgown and wrapper, he walked over and held his hands out.

"What is it?" she asked, and he nodded to her hand.

"I'd like to see your injuries."

"Why?"

"To check on them and rewrap the bandage," he said, reaching out and lifting it, turning it one way and the next. "It is certainly bruised," he murmured. "Does it hurt?"

"Only if I bump it into anything," she said. "Otherwise it is fine."

"Can I rewrap it?" he asked, and she nodded.

"Very well."

He sat on the edge of the bed, patting the blankets next to him and she took a seat. He tugged her hand into his lap, and Faith inhaled sharply at the hard length of his thigh against hers. He certainly didn't provide her with much space, but then, neither did he push her toward anything further than she was comfortable with, which she appreciated.

He had, so far, been a gentleman – which was more than she could have asked for, especially considering that he hadn't agreed to her accompanying him on this journey until it was too late.

Eric was gentle as he unwrapped the bandage from her hand and then carefully washed the cuts below before wrapping it in a clean bandage.

"Thank you," she said, and he nodded.

"Hopefully it shall heal quickly. You are a healthy young woman."

"Not that young," she muttered, but he waved away her words.

"Well, you are a married woman now," he teased, and she rolled her eyes.

"For a few weeks," she said.

"True," he said, unrolling the blankets down next to the bed again.

"Eric," she said with a sigh, "you cannot sleep there again."

"Why not?" he asked.

"Because you were obviously in pain last night."

"Why would you think that?" he asked indignantly.

"I appreciate your attempts to make it seem as though you were fine, but I could tell that the floorboards hurt you, the way you were limping around the room this morning," she said. "Surely there must be a better situation."

"I cannot exactly see one," he said.

"You could..." she cleared her throat. "You could sleep on the bed with me."

"No," he said swiftly, surprising her. Here she thought he would think that to be a phenomenal idea. "I cannot."

"Why not?" she asked, somewhat affronted.

"It just... it just would not be good," he said, shaking his head as he stood and began to back away. "Can you just trust me on this?"

"Not to worry," she said. "I will not try to seduce you and trick you into marriage."

He let out a bark of laughter at that, backing away further from her. She smiled at first until she realized just *how* humorous he found the idea.

"I'm sorry," she said, "I fail to see why the thought is so absurd."

He reached out, placing a hand on her knee. "Because," he said, "if it was up to me, we would have been married years ago."

"What?" she said, sitting back sharply at his admission, astonished. "How can you say that?"

"I was ready to marry you, then," he said with a sigh. "It was you that decided you wanted nothing more to do with me."

Right. Because of what she had seen.

"I thought I was nothing more than a tryst to you. One of many women."

"You were so much more."

She took a breath, telling herself not to give in to his charms.

"Tell me this," she said, turning toward him and bringing her legs up on the bed, crossing one ankle over the other, "If we had married, would you have been true to me?"

"True to you?"

"Yes," she said. "Would you have taken any other women?"

"No," he said vehemently, shaking his head. "Of course not."

"You, Lord Ferrington, Eric Rowley, seducer of all women, would be satisfied with only one woman for the rest of your life?"

"Yes," he said with no hint of doubt. "If that woman was you." He leaned in closer to her. "Why can you not see what an amazing woman you are, Faith?"

"I—"

"Do not say it," he said, placing a finger over her lips. "I don't want to hear your denial. But I can promise you this. Until you believe it yourself, I will continue to tell you, for every day that we are together."

"Why?" she asked, bewildered.

"Because it is the truth, and you deserve to hear it," he said. "Now, time for bed."

"Sleep on the bed," she said, patting the mattress beside her and he nodded once, curtly.

Faith, still bewildered at his words, shuffled to the farthest side of the bed. Fortunately, Eric lay down on top of the blankets beside her, using the one from the floor to cover himself. He was such a large man that he took up nearly the entirety of the bed, even though she could tell he was trying to provide her as much room as he could.

"Comfortable?" he asked, his voice rumbling over the mattress.

"Yes," she said, as she huddled into the blankets. They were thinner than she was used to, and she was a bit chilly, even with her wrapper still on.

"Are you cold?"

"No," she said, but she couldn't hide the slight shiver that overcame her.

She was facing the wall but felt him turn over in the bed, and suddenly she sensed a large arm hovering over her head.

"Come here."

"I shouldn't."

"Do you want to?"

She couldn't answer that aloud – for yes, she did. Very much so. And for more reason than simply warmth, although that was a bonus.

Finally, she gave in, scooting backward until her back was touching his chest, and his large arm wrapped around her, tugging her in tighter.

Faith was rigid against him, uncertain at this new sensation. She was not particularly affectionate and could not remember the last time she had embraced anyone besides her sister or her mother.

"Relax," he murmured in her ear. "We are just sleeping. I promise."

Not long afterward, his breath became slow and she realized with a start that he was already asleep. What must it be like to be able to sleep so easily? It took her forever to settle into bed each night.

Still, his even breath calmed her, and before long she found herself relaxing into him, accepting his warmth and comfort.

The next thing she knew, it was morning.

* * *

Eric stared out over the rail, watching the land slowly become larger in front of them.

It had been a full two weeks since they had begun this journey to San Sebastian. The captain had been accurate in his initial estimate.

But Eric was glad of the length of the journey, for it had turned into two of the best weeks of his life.

Faith, who had quite clearly grown to resent him over the

past few years, seemed to be slowly opening up to him. They had shared moments of laughter, she had let down a few of her walls, and she had accepted, at least, his friendship.

He hadn't realized how much he had missed her since she had decided she no longer wanted him in her life. He might have met other women, but none of them had been Faith, as much as he had always wished that there would be another who could take her place in his heart and in his head.

As far as he could tell, everyone aboard the ship believed their tale that they were husband and wife. None of the men had again attempted anything with Faith, although Eric had made sure that she was always in his sights, even when she was spending time with Patricia, whom she had befriended, or reading alone in her – their – room. Her hand had healed and he had only caught a glimpse of Mr. Smith from across the ship.

"There it is."

Eric turned when Faith's voice met his ear beside him, her fresh lemon scent intermingling with the spray of the ocean. He had seen her bar of soap beside the washbasin and could admit to using it himself a few times as he enjoyed it so much.

"Spain," he murmured. "So close yet so far."

"When one must avoid the country between, yes."

Eric turned around, leaning back on the rail so that he could more closely admire her. She had continued to allow him to hold her at night, and he could admit how much he enjoyed the mornings when he woke up with her head on his chest, her hand splayed over his abdomen. He always made sure to move before she woke up, in fear that if she realized how she clung to him in sleep she would make him return to the floor.

She hadn't made any suggestion that she would be interested in any further contact with him, even as each night brought him increasing frustration from being so physically close yet unable to act on his desire.

"Are you ready for what is to come next?"

"Searching San Sebastian for a clue or a treasure when we know nothing of where to look?" she shrugged. "Sure."

"That's the spirit," he said, just as the captain called to the crew to prepare to dock.

They had made it to their destination.

Now the question was just what they might find there.

CHAPTER 8

"It is a beautiful place," Faith said, appreciating the vibrant streets of the town as they made their way through, Eric carrying some of their belongings, a hired man behind them with the other two bags.

"It is," he agreed. "We should speak Spanish while we are here unless we know we are completely alone."

"Very well," she said, switching languages. "Is that the inn around the corner?"

"Yes, according to our friend here," he said. "Would be a good place to start – to get settled, find something to eat, and ask the locals some questions about the family."

She nodded and followed him through the front doors, crossing through the tavern to find the innkeeper. Quite a few heads turned their way as they approached, but Eric with his usual brightness greeted them all as though he was meant to be there.

"Eric," Faith began, needing to ask him what their story was, but he was already speaking to the man who came out to greet them.

"Hola, amigo," he said. "My wife and I are going to be here for a time and require a room."

So she was his wife again. She had hoped they would be able to find a different ruse. It was a plausible theory and she supposed she was in no less danger here than she was on the ship, but she found it difficult to keep up the pretense. For one, she could not be as rude to him as she usually was.

She also didn't like that she was somewhat enjoying the idea that the two of them were wed.

"What brings you to San Sebastian?" the innkeeper asked.

"My wife has relations who she believes used to live here," Eric said. "The Palencia family."

That captured the man's attention.

"You don't say? They are a noble family, live just outside the city – when they are in residence," he said.

"What are they like?"

The innkeeper paused, wrinkling his nose as he looked at Faith. "You do not look like any of them. They are dark-haired, olive-skinned."

"My relation goes back generations," she explained. "They likely will not even remember me. I just always so longed to see the home that I heard so much about."

"Oh, yes," he said. "The Palencia manor is stunning – at least, from the outside. Not many of us have ever been within unless working as servants."

"I see," she said. "Do you think I will be welcomed?"

The innkeeper frowned at her. "Truthfully? Likely not."

Faith exchanged a glance with Eric but said nothing further.

"Follow me," the innkeeper said, gesturing forward and they walked behind him up the staircase which overlooked the square courtyard below. "Put you in the end room here," he said. "Planning to stay long?"

"We're not entirely sure yet," Eric said. "Does it matter?"

"Not really, long as you pay," the innkeeper said, fitting a key into the lock and opening up the door.

The room was fairly sparse, but looked comfortable enough, with a washbasin in the corner, a wardrobe, and – of course – the one bed in the middle.

The innkeeper looked them up and down, obviously assessing their finer clothing, although Faith could admit her gown had seen better days before this journey began.

"Do you have servants?"

"Not with us," Eric said.

"Very well. Anything else you need?"

"Yes, actually," Faith said, hoping she wasn't asking for too much but unable to help herself. "I would dearly love a bath if it would be at all possible."

"It will cost you."

"That's fine," Eric said, stepping forward and pressing coins into the innkeeper's hand. "Whatever she'd like."

Faith shot a look at him, wondering if he had any ulterior motive, but his face was the picture of innocence.

The innkeeper promised it would be ready in due time, and Eric and Faith made quick work of organizing their few belongings.

"This is not like any travel I have ever undertaken before," Faith said, looking around the room, her hands on her hips.

"You have stayed in inns before, have you not?" he asked.

"Yes, I have," she said. "But not for an extended amount of time. Usually just for a night when stopping while travelling."

"Perhaps with your charm, we will be invited to stay at the estate," he said with a grin, and she couldn't help but roll her eyes at him, knowing that, if anything, it would be he who would gain them entrance.

There was a knock at the door a few minutes later, and two men appeared with a large washbasin, followed by maids with boiling buckets of water. It took a few trips, but eventually, a steaming bath awaited Faith. She had never been so grateful for a tub of water before.

"I'll wait outside," Eric said, and she nodded her thanks before he left the room, likely to look over the courtyard below.

Faith undressed and then sunk into the water, closing her eyes at the bliss that enveloped her. After a few moments of languidness, she leaned out to pick up her soap but found that it was too far from her reach.

"Blast it," she said, trying to stretch her arm out as far as she could to where it sat on the table. If she pushed off enough, she could reach farther and perhaps... "ah!" she couldn't stop herself from crying out when her foot slipped and she splashed back down into the tub, water sloshing over the sides as her head dipped under its surface.

When she came up sputtering a few moments later, she rubbed her eyes, wiped the water off of her face – and found two very brown, very concerned eyes staring back at her.

* * *

ERIC HAD BEEN STANDING OUTSIDE of the room, looking over the balcony at all of the activity occurring in the courtyard below, which never disappointed. Hopefully, he and Faith would be able to sleep.

Although, come to think of it, he had been sleeping rather well with Faith by his side.

He hadn't even considered providing the innkeeper with another story regarding their travelling situation. The only other way they could do so without causing scandal was to name themselves brother and sister, but he would rather not.

Not that it mattered for no one had any awareness of their identity here – which made their current story all the more plausible.

Truth be told, he had been trying to distract himself from picturing his fake wife inside, her naked body dipping beneath the warm water, her hands lathing soap over her soft skin.

He hadn't been faring very well in his endeavour when he had heard her shout followed by the splash, and he had pushed into the room to check on her without even thinking.

When he had seen her fully submerged beneath the water, he had dashed over to the tub and was just about to reach in when she surfaced.

"Eric!" she cried out when she opened her eyes to find him there. "What are you doing?"

"The better question is what are *you* doing?" He knew he shouldn't be taking such an angry tone with her, but his worry for her had overtaken all rational thought. "I thought you were drowning!"

"In a bathtub?" she asked in disbelief, droplets of water dripping from her eyelashes, which made him all the more irate.

"Yes, in a bathtub! People frequently drown in bathtubs. You could have hit your head and slipped underwater. How would I have known?"

"Well, I am fine," she said. "I am also not exactly... decent."

It was only then that he realized he could see her shape through the water. He couldn't exactly see details but it was very easy to imagine them. And the way the tops of her breasts were bobbing overtop of the water...

"Eric!"

He hadn't been discreet in his perusal.

"I am sorry. I truly am," he said, backing away. "I never meant... it's just that you... I couldn't help—"

She surprised him with the laugh that emerged. "I am not sure that I have ever known you to be without words before.

Perhaps the stories are not true, if this is what a naked woman does to you."

He couldn't meet her eyes then, for it was not as though the stories were false, it was just that none of the other naked women were her. A naked Faith was an altogether different story.

Besides that, he knew what to expect from other women. With Faith…

He cleared his throat. "Now that I see you are just fine, I will leave you. Again. Do not scare me like that, please."

As much as everything within him was begging him to stay, he turned around and made for the door as fast as he could, before he did something he shouldn't – something he was very certain he would regret.

"Eric?"

Well, that stopped him mid-track.

"Yes?" he said without turning around.

"I slipped because I was reaching for the soap. It is still too far. Do you think you could pass it to me?"

He passed a hand over his eyes. Oh, was he being tempted today. He supposed he deserved it, but this was about to break him.

"Of course," he said, hearing the strain in his voice. He looked back and saw the soap – that lemon soap that haunted him – sitting there on the washbasin. He grabbed it and passed it to her quickly, nearly dropping it in his haste.

He could tell that she was laughing at him – enjoying this, even. The little minx. She wasn't so innocent after all, was she?

"Thank you," she said, her voice soft and velvety, and he nodded and walked out the door, although one thing was for certain – he would never forget the way she looked in the water – nor the way it made him feel.

Never.

* * *

Faith could have languished in the bathtub for hours, but, of course, the water grew colder and she eventually had to emerge.

She dressed as best she could before opening the door and telling Eric she was finished. He came in without a word, deftly fastening the back of her gown for her.

"I suppose we can ask them to come and empty the tub now," she said, and he shook his head.

"I'll quickly wash first."

Guilt filled her at the amount of time she had taken within. "The water is cold!"

"No matter," he said, but she bit her lip anyway, wondering if the man had ever had a cold bath in his life. If he said he was fine, though, then so be it.

"I shall leave for you," she said, taking a step away, but he stopped her, a steely edge to his voice.

"Absolutely not."

"But—"

"Faith, it is not safe for you to be alone," he said, obviously trying for patience. "Have you not already learned that?"

She felt properly chastised but annoyed even so.

She sighed. "Very well," she said, moving to the side of the room, lifting her book off of the nightstand as she took a seat with her back to him, her spine sternly lifted. "Please tell me when you are finished."

She heard the rustling of his clothes, the splash of the water when he entered, and the yelp he tried to muffle when he realized just how cold it was.

Faith laughed slightly, but it was difficult to find too much humor in the situation.

For the truth was, being here with him, in this room, as

he bathed was causing a commotion within her, one that – were she being honest – scared her.

She could remember Eric's kiss as though it just happened, and the more time they spent together, the more she forgot about his womanizing ways.

But she best remember, or else she could find herself back where she began – broken-hearted. A situation she never wanted to find herself in again.

There was one idea, however, that began to niggle at her. One that suggested maybe, just maybe, she could have fun and satisfy her urges without giving away her heart.

Her body liked that idea. Even if her head told her it would never work.

She just had no idea which one would win out.

CHAPTER 9

"This is rather grand," Faith said, staring up at the estate. She was certainly familiar with homes of this stature, but not in this style with Castillo de la Lunca's stuccoed siding, clay tile roof held up by columns. A balcony with a wrought-iron railing surrounded the top, statues of gargoyles overlooking the ocean beyond.

"Reminds me of Newfield," Eric said, referring to her family's own country home, which was similarly situated on the coast.

"This is lusher," she murmured, looking around the grounds. "It seems to fit within its surroundings."

"That it does," he said, and she didn't miss the way his eyes ran down her figure. At first, she had thought he was doing so to disconcert her, but she could tell he wasn't doing so on purpose – which meant that he actually did appreciate how she looked. She wasn't sure what exactly to do with that information.

"Best get this over with," he said, stepping up and knocking on the door.

A tall, broad, and sombre servant answered momentarily,

and Faith laced her hand through Eric's elbow. To sell their story, of course – for no other reason. While she didn't miss the look he gave her when he did so, she chose to ignore it for now.

"Can I help you?"

"Yes," Eric said. "My wife and I are here from Madrid. She is a distant relative of the Palencia family and would like to pay her regards."

The butler looked Faith up and down with suspicion but told them he would return momentarily. They waited in the wide foyer, looking around with interest.

"Does it appear particularly well-kept to you?" Faith murmured in Eric's ear. He shook his head as he looked around at torn wallpaper, crumbled brick, and tarnished brass.

"It looks to me like they have fallen into as hard of times as the Sutcliffe family," he whispered back.

"At least the Sutcliffes do their best to make Castleton appealing," she said lowly. "It appears this family has given up on all pretenses."

"Which tells us that they most certainly have not found this treasure themselves," he said, both of them straightening when the butler reappeared.

"The *marqués* and *marquesa* are not currently in residence," he said. "However, their son is and he would be pleased to meet with you. If you would follow me to the drawing room?"

The house was eerily silent as they walked through, and it took Faith a moment to realize what was missing – people. Even if there were few of them in residence at home, there were always servants about. They had walked through three rooms and so far, there was no sign of another servant save the butler whom they were currently following.

He opened the door to a drawing room, which had a

musty feel to it, before he left them, and soon enough the door opened once more to admit a tall, slim young man near their age. He had a pointed beard and a mustache which curled slightly at the end, giving him a somewhat sinister look.

His dark eyes flicked around the room until they landed on Faith and then his lips turned up into a smile.

"Good afternoon," he said. "My butler tells me that you are distant relatives. I am eager to learn more about you. You may call me *Don* Raphael."

He sat down across from them, crossing one leg over the other as he rested his chin on his fist.

"Thank you for inviting us into your home, *Don* Raphael. My great-grandmother was once the *Dona* Palencia," Faith said, telling the story that Cassandra had told her, taking on her friend's identity for the moment. "She left San Sebastian and began a new family."

Don Raphael leaned forward, his eyes narrowing. "Is this the traitor that left us for the English duke?"

Faith and Eric exchanged a glance. This was not exactly going to plan.

"I have not heard anything about the English," Faith said slowly. "My great-grandmother moved to Madrid. That is where we are from."

"Is the family folklore mistaken, then?" *Don* Raphael asked, although from the expression on his face, it was clear he didn't believe it.

"Perhaps," Faith said.

"So, what brings you here?" *Don* Raphael said, and that's when Eric joined the conversation.

"My wife and I are recently married," he said, reaching out and joining his hand with Faith's, sending a tremor through her body from where their fingers touched. She couldn't deny it any longer. This man affected every part of her. "We decided to go on a holiday in San Sebastian, and since we were here, she wanted to meet her distant relatives and learn more about where her great-grandmother was from."

"Exactly," Faith said, wishing the tales would roll off of her tongue as easily.

"Well, I would certainly be more interested in hearing about you and what happened with your family," *Don* Raphael said. "Although, from what you tell me, I do not believe we would have any relation."

"Oh?" Faith said, uncertain now, trying to remember Cassandra's family tree. From what she could remember, Cassandra's great-grandmother had been the one to come to England, after she was widowed – but of course. That would mean that her first husband's brother would have continued the Palencia family line and would be *Don* Raphael's ancestor.

"Yes," he said, his smile widening. "Although I would be more than happy to learn more about you, Mrs.…"

"Sanchez."

"Mrs. Sanchez," he said with a quick look over at Eric. Fortunately, Eric's coloring was dark enough for him to pass for a Spaniard. *Don* Raphael did not seem to have any particular interest in him, although he might wonder about Faith. He cleared his throat before returning his attention to Faith.

"As it happens, I have an engagement that I must attend shortly. Where are you staying?"

"At the inn," Eric said, leaning back with his arms crossed over his chest.

"Oh," *Don* Raphael said, a look of displeasure crossing his face. "That will never do. You must stay here."

"Oh, we couldn't," Faith said quickly, shaking her head. She had been the guest at many a home before, but it didn't seem right to stay at this house – they were using this man to try to find a treasure that his family could, potentially, have equal claim to.

"On the contrary, Mrs. Sanchez," he said, leaning forward toward her. "I would be more than happy to have you here."

Eric cleared his throat and leaned forward himself, even as he clasped Faith's hand tighter than he had before.

"And am I also welcome, *Don* Raphael?" he asked, with more edge to his voice than Faith was used to hearing.

"Of course, Mr. Sanchez," *Don* Raphael said with a smile that did not at all appear genuine crossing his face. "Now, why do you not arrange for your belongings to be sent here? I will not be here tonight but I look forward to hosting you tomorrow. We can spend the day touring the estate and then we can enjoy dinner together."

"That sounds perfect," Faith said with a smile. "Shall we go collect our things, dear?"

The endearment sounded disingenuous even to her ears, but *Don* Raphael didn't seem to question it, although she could tell that Eric was trying not to laugh.

"Very well," Eric said. "Thank you for your generous offer. I can assure you that my *wife* and I will not overstay your hospitality."

"Stay as long as you'd like," *Don* Raphael said, and, as if magically summoned, the butler appeared. "Abello will show you out."

They parted ways with *Don* Raphael outside of the drawing room door, and Faith decided that perhaps the servant could provide some information.

"Tell me, Abello, have you served the Palencia family long?"

"All my life," he said in a low, sombre voice. "My family has been with the Palencia family for generations."

"Is that so?" she asked, an eyebrow rising. "Perhaps they knew my great-grandmother, then."

THE LORD'S COMPASS

"Likely," was all he said. He was not the talkative type.

"Perhaps someone in your family might remember," Eric said, but Abello ignored the comment.

"When you return, I shall show you to your chambers," he said. "Farewell."

And with that, he closed the entrance door behind them.

"Well, what do you make of that?" Faith asked Eric as he led her down the drive. He still had her hand clasped tightly within his and didn't seem to have any inkling of releasing it as he tugged her away from the house.

"That was… interesting," he said. "I do not like the idea of staying at this place."

"Why?" she asked, looking at him with interest. "It provides us with the perfect opportunity to search the grounds and estate and learn more about where the treasure may be."

But Eric was shaking his head, his face hard. "I didn't like the way he looked at you."

"The way he looked at me?" Faith's mouth dropped open. "Why Eric, are you… are you jealous?"

He glanced at her quickly before he faced the path in front of them once more. "As far as he is aware, you are my wife. He should not be looking at you like that."

"And that is all?"

"What else would there be?"

He grunted his response, and Faith had to keep from laughing. The man was usually so eloquent.

"I didn't like the feel of the place," he finally said. "It was creepy."

"It did have a sombre air to it," she admitted. "But it was the lack of servants and its disrepair. It felt empty."

"It was more than that."

"You know nothing about it!" she scoffed.

"It's a feeling," he said with a shrug. "Sometimes that is the best direction to follow."

Faith scoffed, "Feelings are not facts."

"That is where we disagree."

"Very well," she said as they re-entered the town itself. "But you must admit this is a better opportunity than we could have asked for."

"Perhaps," he acquiesced. "But do you not think that if there was a clue to be found, they would have discovered it already? They certainly have not located any treasure of significance."

"Perhaps they do not know what they are looking for," she said.

"Speaking of looking – he's watching us."

"Who?"

"*Don* Raphael, through the window. Don't look up."

He wrapped his hands around her elbows, squeezed tight, and pulled her in toward him.

"Trust me," he said, his voice breathless.

And then he kissed her.

CHAPTER 10

He took her breath away. When his lips descended on hers, she paused in a moment of shock before she melted into him without thought, the Palencia manor, *Don* Raphael, and San Sebastian itself fading away as she had only one thought – Eric and his touch.

His lips brushed against hers softly at first, the kiss tender, intimate. He cradled her head in one of his large hands as the other splayed across her back, drawing her close. Their breath mingled, creating a delicate moment, until his kiss deepened, more fervent.

Faith wondered if every kiss was like this – two people moving in perfect harmony, exploring and savoring the taste of one another. A soft, contented sigh escaped her lips at just how talented Eric was at this.

Which was the very thought that had her jumping back and away from him. He was talented because he was practiced. This had nothing to do with her.

"Sorry," he murmured. "Just had to convince *Don* Raphael that we are who we say we are – husband and wife."

"Of course," she said, turning away, trying to prevent

herself from bringing her fingers to her lips, where he had left an indelible mark – and a craving for more.

* * *

Eric knew that if anyone was asked to describe him, they would say that he was friendly. Jovial. Happy.

But a few hours after the kiss he had seized in an opportune moment, he was not happy. Not at all.

He knew he should be. He knew that the worst-case scenario would have been for them to be turned away at the door of Castillo de la Luna with no avenue to access the manor and search for what could potentially be a clue.

But as he sat in the cold bedchamber – alone – in a manor that he would bet was filled with ghosts who had died in the most atrocious of ways, he had no ounce of happiness within him.

The worst part of it was that staying at this estate meant that he was no longer in a chamber with Faith, as two chambers had been prepared for them. How fortuitous. At least the rooms were attached.

And then, of course, there had been the kiss. The kiss that he told her had meant nothing but, in actuality, was everything to him. He had seen his chance and he had taken it. But she had not seemed pleased.

"Faith?" he called out now, and she appeared in the doorway between their bedrooms momentarily.

"I thought we were to speak Spanish," she said in a loud whisper.

"We are alone here," he said, holding his hands up. "Or do you think the plethora of servants are going to overhear and come racing in?"

"It is rather odd, isn't it, that there are hardly any here? No wonder the house is falling down. Why, I would wager this room has not changed since Cassandra's great-grandmother lived here."

"Likely not," he said, staring at the worn bedding and the dark paintings on the crimson walls that were covered with a layer of dust.

"Be sure to leave the door between our rooms open," he said, walking toward her, and she looked up at him, her hair falling back over her neck as she was still preparing for dinner, even though it sounded like it would just be the two of them attending.

"Why?"

"For safety."

"There is no one here to attack me. I shall be perfectly fine," she insisted, and he raised a brow.

"Are you so sure of that?"

"Why must you be so ornery?"

"Ornery?" he straightened, affronted. "No one has ever called me ornery before."

"Well," she said, "I must simply bring out the best in you."

She returned to her room to finish her preparations, not reappearing until she needed help fastening her gown.

"Thank you," she murmured, even as he purposefully closed the fastenings ever so slowly, despite his ability to complete it much quicker. He had always been in pursuit of her, yes, but the more time they spent together, the more he enjoyed having her with him. He hadn't yet decided just what he was going to do about it, but one thing was for certain – if he was going to suffer from unfulfilled lust, then so was she.

He offered his arm to her as they left the room, following the labyrinth of stairs and corridors, taking a few wrong turns along the way until they emerged in what appeared to be the dining room. Two solitary candles standing in the middle of the table provided the only light. Places were set at opposite ends of the long table, which Eric took one look at before he shook his head and moved one place setting beside the other, positioning the candles right in front of them.

"Can we do that?" Faith asked, and Eric shrugged.

"Why not? Our host said he was not joining us tonight."

"Do you not find that odd?" she asked, taking a seat when Eric pulled her chair out for her, as there were no footmen about unless they were hiding in the corners that were so dark they couldn't quite make them out. "Where else would he go? I cannot imagine there would be much to do in San Sebastian after dark."

"This entire situation is odd," he said. "But we are deep in it now, so we best follow through."

"Dinner is served."

They both visibly jumped at the sudden appearance of the butler behind them.

"Abello!" Eric said, recovering first. "Good to see a familiar face."

Abello placed a bowl of soup – well, clear liquid with a few vegetables floating within it – in front of each of them.

"Abello, if I might ask," Faith said cautiously, "is there no one else to serve dinner?"

"The house is usually uninhabited," he said without expression. "There is only me, the maid who is also the cook, and a groundskeeper."

"For an estate this size?" Eric exclaimed, and Abello turned an eye on him that did not mask his indignation at the question.

"We are efficient."

"You must be," Eric said, before leaning in conspiratorially. "I am sure you would appreciate more help, though."

"Are you offering?"

Ah, Abello had some humor within him after all.

Eric chuckled. "I am afraid I would only hinder you," he

said. "But I can put in a good word with your employer, if you'd like, see if he has any plans to add more staff."

Abello said nothing as he poured wine into their glasses and then departed, leaving them alone once more.

"What are you doing?" Faith hissed. "He told us his family has been here for generations. He is not going to share with us any information on his employers! I am sure he is not taking kindly to us offering our opinions."

"You are right," Eric said with a sigh. "Perhaps we might have more luck with other servants."

They cautiously ate their meal, which one would not call delicious but also not exactly horrific.

Dessert was two sad pieces of pineapple on a plate.

Eric frowned as he stared at them. "Do you suppose they have poisoned us?"

Faith's mouth gaped open as she dropped her fork, the clatter resounding about the room.

"Why would you say that now, after we have just finished eating?"

He shrugged. "It just occurred to me."

"Do you ever consider what you are about to say before you say it?"

"No," he said immediately and then laughed. "I didn't even think that through, did I?"

Her lips moved in something he considered just might be a prayer, and then Abello re-entered. Damn, but the large man moved with the silence of a cat.

"I hope all was satisfactory."

"Of course," Eric said, before glancing at Faith and then back at the butler. "Say, could we perhaps thank the cook?"

"She is not dressed to meet you."

"Oh, that's fine, we are not particularly concerned, are we, sweetheart?"

"No, *dear*, we are not," Faith returned.

"Very well," Abello said, although displeased.

A few moments later, he returned to the room, followed by a young woman, her head bowed before them.

"Lola," he said, pointing to her, and then stepped back.

"Lola, that was exemplary," Eric said, earning himself a look from Faith which suggested he was overselling it, as even Lola was likely aware it was far from that. He cleared his throat. "Where did you learn to cook?"

"My mother," she said in what was near to a whisper, as she was obviously not used to being addressed by those she served.

"Well, she did a fine job," he said with his most winning smile, one which nearly always worked on women. "How long have you worked here?"

"A few months," she said.

"Do you enjoy it?"

"Lola," Abello said, stepping forward. "Back to the kitchen."

She nodded, curtsying slightly before leaving the room.

As Eric and Faith rose from the table, Faith leaned into him, her breath tickling his neck. He would have enjoyed it except that he was quite ticklish there and he couldn't help but flinch. "What was that about?" she asked.

"Just trying to get closer to the staff, hoping to learn something."

She nodded. "Let me try something." She turned around and spoke in a louder tone. "Abello, do you suppose Lola could spare a few moments to help me undress?"

"I shall send her up," he said, and Faith shot Eric a triumphant smile as they exited through the door.

"I will have a chat with her, woman to woman."

"Do women trust you?" he couldn't help but ask, and she looked at him sharply.

"What is that supposed to mean?"

"Nothing," he bluffed. "You are most charming."

"I have charmed you, haven't I?" she asked, raising a brow and he sighed, shaking his head.

"Apparently," he sighed. "I just wish I knew how."

That earned him a swat before they entered their rooms, but she was laughing, at least.

He'd take it.

* * *

"THANK YOU VERY MUCH, Lola. I do appreciate your assistance," Faith said when the maid entered her room to help her. Faith had made sure that the door was closed between her chamber and Eric's, for she wanted Lola to feel free to share without any reservations. She sensed that the girl was intimidated by Eric, and Faith didn't blame her – Eric might put people at ease, but he could also be an overwhelming presence.

"Of course, my lady," she said.

"My husband" –now there was something she never thought she would say, especially about Eric— "can sometimes be a bit too friendly and forward. I hope he did not make you feel uncomfortable."

Lola met her eyes in the mirror as she removed the pins from Faith's hair.

"Not at all," she said. "It is only that I have not cooked long so I was unsure if it was satisfactory. There was also very little in the stores so I did the best I could—"

She clamped her lips together suddenly as though realizing she had, perhaps, said too much.

"I understand," Faith said, pretending that she had said nothing of significance. "*Don* Raphael was not expecting us, so how could he have been prepared?"

Faith hoped she sounded compassionate. She was usually

much more direct, but she tried to imagine that she was speaking to her sister, Hope, who was more emotional in her responses, causing Faith to have to be more careful of how she spoke to her.

"Yes," Lola said, but her gaze dipped, telling Faith that there was more to this story.

"Do you enjoy cooking?" Faith attempted.

"I do," Lola said. "It is usually just for the few servants, however."

"I see," Faith said. "Has there been the same number of servants since you began?"

"Yes."

"Well, hopefully, if the family stays in residence they might add more staff so that you can have more company," Faith said in what she hoped was a cheerful voice.

"I believe there will be more staff if the family is ever able to restore their fortunes. They have gambled most of it away."

"I am sorry to hear it," Faith said, her words true.

"Yes, well, when the lords spend more time away from their estates, having their fun, it makes it hard for them to know what is needed," she said, warming to her topic. "But *Don* Raphael has been here a great deal lately."

"I can see why, as the property is so beautiful," Faith said.

"Truth be told…" Lola said slowly, her gaze meeting Faith's again, "will this stay between us, my lady?"

"Of course," Faith said, her lie slight for the only other person she would tell would be Eric. Now that she had opened the door with Lola, there was no stopping the flood of information.

"*Don* Raphael is looking for something."

"Is he?"

She nodded slowly. "Something worth a lot. He told us

he'll hire more staff when he finds it, so we should keep an eye out for it."

"What are you looking for?" Faith asked, attempting nonchalance. "Maybe we can help."

"No," Lola said quickly. "He can't know I told you about this. Neither can Abello."

"I promise I will not say a thing," Faith said, holding her palms up. "You seem like a lovely young woman, Lola, and I just do not want to see you working so hard."

"Thank you," Lola said quietly. "I think what he's looking for is in the house or on the grounds. A treasure, maybe, though that sounds crazy."

"Crazier things have happened," Faith said with a smile. "If you can unfasten my gown, I can do the rest myself, Lola. Thank you so much."

When the maid left, Faith walked into Eric's bedroom, opening the door without knocking.

"Eric, Lola has—"

She stopped abruptly, for she was in too much shock to continue.

For there was Eric, lounging back on the bed, as naked as could be.

CHAPTER 11

Eric had jumped when the door opened.

But his surprise was worth Faith's expression when she took a good look at him.

"I-I'm sorry," she said, slowly backing away. "I should have knocked. I was just—that is I—I was going to tell you about Lola. What she said, that is. I—I'm just going to go."

When she whirled around, he stood, lifting his wrapper off of the chair next to him.

"No need, I'll cover myself," he said, although he didn't rush to get dressed. Oh, how much fun they could have together if she would let go of some of her reservations. "Tell me about Lola."

When Faith turned around, it took everything within him not to comment on the bright pink of her cheeks, but he said nothing as she told him of her conversation.

"So they know there is a treasure," he said, stroking his chin. "Interesting."

"Do you think the actual treasure is here?" she asked. "And if we find it – would we be stealing it?"

He took her hand and tugged her over to the bed, sitting

down next to her on it. He kept her warm hands between his as he looked into her eyes.

"At this point, we are just helping our friends. I say we find out what we can, and then let Ashford and Lady Covington decide what they want to do as it is their family who is involved. Is that fair?"

She nodded. "I suppose."

He waited for her to say something else, to show any inkling that she was interested in what more could come from this opportunity that was placed between the two of them, but she stood abruptly and began to back away.

"Goodnight, Eric. Sleep well."

Then she was practically racing from the room, the flaps of her dress opening and closing like wings behind her.

* * *

FAITH COULDN'T SLEEP that night and it was all Eric's fault.

It was primarily that he had practically invited her to see him naked. Why the man couldn't cover himself, she had no idea, although she supposed that with a body like his, he was happy to show it off.

She wished she could be so open herself, so unashamed to reveal unapologetically who she was.

The noises didn't help ease her to sleep.

The house creaked and groaned. A wind had stirred up outside, and a tree branch continually banged against her window. She wondered if Eric's room was similarly loud.

Then she started to picture him naked again, which made matters even worse.

She was in the middle of chastising herself when the howling began.

At first, she thought it was just the wind whistling. But

then it began to crescendo in earnest until it sounded like someone was standing outside her room, moaning in pain.

Her first instinct was to flee her bed and run to Eric, but she refused to be that woman who needed the help of a man at the first sign of trouble.

Even if that man's arms were strong and quite comforting.

"Faith?"

She jumped, throwing back the covers she had just burrowed herself under.

"Eric?"

The shuffle of feet sounded from their connecting door, which he closed behind him – and then, in what she could only describe as a sprint, he was crossing the room and diving into bed beside her as though the devil himself was chasing him.

He reached out and hauled her in close to him, holding her so tightly against his body that she could feel his rapidly beating heart.

"I came to see if you were scared," he said, his voice breathy, and despite her fear, she couldn't help the laughter that was bubbling up inside of her.

"Why, Eric," she said, "are you... afraid?"

"No," he said quickly – too quickly. "I just told you. I needed to see if you were all right."

"I am just fine," she said, "although that noise is awfully disconcerting. Do you think someone is injured? One of the servants? Oh no, perhaps it is Lola. What could have happened?"

"It could be a ghost," he said in a whisper, as though the ghost could overhear him. "It's like I said when we arrived. I'm sure this place is full of all kinds of terrible, creepy creatures."

"Eric. There is no such thing as ghosts."

"How do you know?"

"I just know."

"You may not believe, but you do not *know* that. No one does."

"Very well," she said, rolling her eyes. "I am not scared of nonexistent ghosts."

"You should be."

"Would it make you feel better if I was?"

"Yes."

"Fine. Thank you for coming to ensure I was well," she said, unable to prevent the laughter in her voice. "I will admit that I am worried someone is in trouble. I think we should go check to make sure that nothing is amiss."

"What?" he exclaimed, sitting upright. "You want us to go out there?"

It was fairly dark in the room, but she was sure he was pointing at the door.

"That would be the only way 'out there,'" she said.

He was already shaking his head. "We are not leaving this room. It is far too dangerous."

Faith, however, was buoyed by his presence and addressing his fear made her more aware of what was the truth and was more likely the reality.

"I fail to see what could be dangerous, but I respect your fear. You stay here. I will go check," she said, swinging her legs off of the bed.

"Faith, you cannot do that. You could get hurt – or worse."

But she was already up out of bed, opening the door and padding down the hallway. "Good evening?" she called. "Is anyone here?"

Hearing no response, she began to back up to try the other direction and let out a shriek when she was met with resistance behind her.

"It's just me," Eric said in a loud whisper. "Hush."

He'd had the foresight to bring a candle, which he lifted to shine around them.

"Nothing looks out of the ordinary," he said with a shrug of his shoulders. "Back to bed, I suppose."

But Faith ignored him, already walking down the stairs. "Just a quick check," she said, reaching the landing as his arm tucked around her waist and he held her against him.

"Are you using me as a shield?" she asked incredulously.

"No!" he exclaimed. "I am making sure you are well protected."

"Then I should be behind you, should I not?"

"No," he said, drawing out the word as though she wasn't smart enough to understand. "I am making sure that you are not attacked from behind."

"You are impossible," she muttered as they moved from room to room on the ground floor. "All is well."

"The howling has stopped," he noted.

"Yes, it stopped once we left the room," she said. "Well, I'm not sure what else is to be done right now. We will have to ask *Don* Raphael tomorrow if this is a regular occurrence."

"Wonderful. Can we go back to bed now?"

"Will you be able to sleep?" she asked jokingly, but when they entered her room, he turned to face her, no smile on his face.

"Not without you," he said, and she bit her lip.

"You shouldn't say those things to me," she muttered.

"Why not?" he asked. "It is the truth. It wouldn't be the first time we have shared a bed. I know it's not exactly proper, but I figure, we're not in England. What happens between us in Spain… can stay in Spain."

He was right except, she couldn't say what it was, but something had changed. Shifted. If they got into that bed together, it wouldn't be because they had to – it would be because they wanted to.

She knew she couldn't have a future with him, but that thought started to nag at her once more – what if they could have some fun, some experiences together that she might never have the opportunity to have again?

Could she separate her body from her feelings?

"Very well," she finally said. "You can sleep in here if you'd like. But just sleep."

"Wonderful," he said with a grin that appeared genuine. Was he truly so happy to simply sleep next to her?

She climbed into bed first, noting that they already seemed to have each claimed a side, no matter if they were on the ship, at the inn, or here at this estate.

She turned to her side, facing the wall, feeling the dip in the bed when he lay down upon it, rolling over until he was tucking her body into his.

"What will you do when we are no longer sharing bedchambers?" she murmured, even as tears frustratingly pricked her eyes at the thought of sleeping alone once more.

"I shall be very lonely," he said with a sigh, and she snorted.

"What am I saying?" she said, unable to help the bitterness that crept in. "You likely never sleep alone."

He was silent for a moment, which she took as agreement from him until he began to speak.

"I cannot say that I am a saint," he said slowly. "But I never actually sleep with any other women."

"What do you mean?" she asked, unable to help the quickening of her heart that perhaps she was different – significant.

"I mean that I never spend an entire night with a woman. We always part ways before the sleeping begins."

Faith didn't respond. For there were two warring factions

within her – the one that was jealous that other women were worth having relations with, and the one that was happy with the fact that there was something special about what she had with Eric.

"Goodnight, Eric," was all she finally said.

"Goodnight, Faith," he said, snuggling in closer to her, his nose and chin nearly nuzzling her neck as his warm breath tickled her cheek.

Before, his presence had caused her comfort and had lulled her to sleep, but the awareness that had been building between them before was creeping over her again. Every place he touched her body – his hand on her hip, his knees in the crook of hers, his chest on her back – seemed to tingle. He shifted slightly back away from her, telling her that he felt it too.

His hand moved from her hip to slide around her waist, his palm splaying across her stomach, and she had to hide her gasp at the warmth that shot from his touch down between her legs.

He was as tense and immobile as she, as they both lay there, likely waiting for it to ebb away.

Finally, Faith couldn't take it any longer.

She turned over to face him, surprised to find his eyes wide and staring when they came face-to-face.

"Is everything all right?" he asked in a strangled voice.

"No," she said. "Not at all. There is something strange between us, and I believe we must determine just what it is."

His throat bobbed as his eyes flicked from one side to the other.

"What's that?" she asked suddenly.

"What's what?" he asked, clearly attempting innocence, but something was protruding into her stomach – something he was trying to hide as he began to shift backward.

"Eric, are you—"

"Ignore it, Faith."

"But—"

"I'm just tired, all right?" he said, rolling his eyes. "It happens when I'm tired."

"Of course," she said, becoming annoyed now, although she wasn't entirely sure why. Was she upset that he didn't want her, that he didn't want to admit he wanted her, or that she wanted him worse than she ever would have imagined? "I am well aware that you do not desire me in that way."

He closed his eyes as though in pain and she began to turn around and draw away from him when he reached out and cupped her shoulder, stopping her.

"Faith."

"Yes?"

"It is not that I do not want you. The truth is, I want you very, very much."

"But—"

"In the time we have been together, we have developed a… truce, you could say. I would even go as far as to call us friends. We haven't had that in years, and I have missed you. I have enjoyed conversing with you without your every word toward me a barbed insult. I do not want to ruin that."

Faith was silent as she finally caught his gaze and held it.

"You scare me," she said quietly.

"As you do me," he answered.

"Perhaps we try something – just to see what happens."

"All right," he said cautiously.

She tilted her face up to his, summoned all of her courage, and kissed him.

CHAPTER 12

*E*ric had kissed many women.
But none had ever compared to Faith.
Which was the very reason why, as much as he wanted her, he had been trying to avoid this. Truly kissing her again, for more than show, would likely ruin him for any other woman in the future.

But when her lips met his, every reservation flew out the window. He was being offered his very dream, the most luscious treat that had ever been presented to him.

And he wasn't fool enough to turn it down.

He meant to briefly return her kiss, long enough that she wouldn't feel rejected but also would not take it as a promise for more.

But the next thing he knew, he had her head in his hands as he angled it just right to accept his kiss, then he dove deep into her mouth and all she had to offer.

He was like a man starved who had been presented with a buffet. His need for her, which had been triggered years ago, suddenly took over his every action as he kissed her with all of the passion he held for her. Her lips were lush, giving, and he licked his way into her mouth, tangling her tongue with his.

She clung to him as she gave in return in equal measure, and soon one of his hands was roaming lower, exploring the swell of her bottom, the indent of her waist.

He ran his hand up her stomach until it reached the plump edge of her breast, and he took his time in lifting it in his hand, cupping it as he brushed his thumb over her nipple. She moaned into his mouth as she pressed herself against him. Eric couldn't ever remember being so on edge from just kissing, touching a woman.

To answer her rocking against him, he lifted her nightgown, pressing his bare leg between her thighs, and she began to ride it, likely purely based on instinct. He let her use him as he tweaked her nipple between his fingers while he didn't break their kiss – for he didn't want her to overthink this, but simply allow herself the pleasure that she deserved.

"Eric," she moaned as she threw her head back, and he knew she was close.

He reached down, pressing his thumb to her button – and she clenched him hard, with her grip, her legs, her heart.

When she finally opened her eyes, they were searching, her breath coming in quick pants as she stared at him in shock.

He managed a goofy smile for her.

"How was that?" he asked, even as he ached.

"That was... indescribable," she said, and he saw when the reservation washed over her. "I am so sorry. I wasn't thinking. I was—"

"Perfect," he said smugly. "That is a feat indeed if I could turn off that brilliant mind of yours."

"Yes, but—"

"Faith," he said, reaching out and tapping her on the nose with his index finger, "I just want to see you happy. You have to believe that. I'll give you whatever you need, and right now, I think you needed that."

"But you—"

"I'm fine."

She met his eye. "I feel that we are no longer even with one another. I would like you to experience the same. I will not be able to sleep otherwise."

"Well," he said, swallowing hard. "I would not want to ruin your sleep."

"Exactly," she said, smiling triumphantly, reaching out a hand.

"I can do it," he said, waving her away, and her face fell.

"You do not want me to—"

"It is not that I do not *want* you, Faith," he said. "It is that if you touch me at this point, I will only last a second or two. And you are worth savoring."

Her mouth formed a round O.

"Can I watch, then?"

Somehow that was nearly as erotic as her stroking him herself, but he couldn't say no to her request.

He backed away slightly as he reached down and took his cock in his hand, keeping her stare as he moved back and forth.

Her eyes dropped to watch him, and he couldn't help a smile of satisfaction when her breath hitched.

"Do you like what you see?" he asked in a low voice.

"I suppose," she said, and he appreciated the fact that she was never coy but rather said exactly what she was thinking.

He knew he wasn't going to last long, and when she covered his hand with her own, moving with him, he groaned in defeat as he began to spend on his wrapper that was lying on the bed below them. Through the slits in his eyelids, he saw Faith's face flushing again as a glossy sheen covered her eyes and her pink lips dropped open.

"That was… intriguing," she said, and he lifted his brows.

"It was?"

"Very much so," she said, as he rolled away from her and cleaned everything up around them, throwing his wrapper on the floor.

"There is more where that came from," he said. "But not tonight. Tonight, we have to sleep."

"You're not scared anymore?" she said, her lips curling up into a smile.

"I believe you have chased my worries away," he said. "Now come here."

She backed up into him, resuming their usual position. The tension had dissipated, leaving in its wake not the awkwardness that he had been concerned about, but rather comfort.

His only fear now? How much he was going to miss this once it was gone.

* * *

THE HOUSE WAS a bit brighter in the morning light, although there were still strange shadows cast about the property that had the hairs on the back of Faith's neck standing up.

"I told you there are ghosts," Eric whispered in her ear as they descended the stairs together.

Faith had awoken with her cheek resting firmly on Eric's hard, muscled chest. She had kept her eyes closed a few moments longer after she awoke, enjoying the moment before he knew what she was doing.

They had fallen into their morning routine of preparing themselves for the day, and now leaving the room and walking down together felt comfortable. Almost too comfortable.

She was the one who had taken the next step forward,

however. He had only followed her lead – meaning she had only her traitorous body to blame.

Although she must admit that she had liked the result of her little experiment. Guilt nibbled at her, telling her that this was wrong, that it was nothing a young lady should be doing.

But perhaps, for once in her life, she was allowed a little bit of fun.

Eric, of course, took everything in stride, acting his usual jovial self – albeit slightly subdued due to their current whereabouts.

"There is no such thing as ghosts," she turned and whispered back, her breath on his neck causing his shoulder to rise as he shivered, and she smiled smugly.

"You did that on purpose," he accused her.

"Did what?" she asked innocently.

"You know I am ticklish there," he grumbled. "I will find your ticklish spot."

"I don't have one."

"You must."

She lifted one shoulder. "Try all you'd like."

"Oh, I will," he said, grinning at her now before he leaned in close and lowered his voice. "And I will have great fun doing so."

Faith was both scandalized and…excited. Flushed.

Oh, this man was a problem.

"There you are!"

They turned to see their host walking out of the breakfast room, his hands clasped together. "Come, join me."

They followed him in, taking a seat at the small, round breakfast table. Faith was used to large spreads on side tables, but here there were just a few loaves in the middle of the table with different types of fruit spreads, as well as a pot of coffee. She would have loved a cup of tea but knew better than to ask. That would all but label her British.

"I assume you are making yourselves at home?" he asked.

"We appreciate your hospitality very much," Eric said. "How was your engagement yesterday?"

Don Raphael's smile broke just for a moment – long enough for them to see what was underneath the mask. It was dark. And frustrated.

"All went well. Thank you for asking," he said as his façade was reconstructed, though he did not share anything further with them. "Now, are you prepared for our tour today?"

"Very much so," Faith said with a nod.

After their brief breakfast, the tour started, their host walking in front of them, not having a particularly great deal of information on the history of the home. He shared the perfunctory details of each room, but when Faith asked about some of the paintings, he said only that they had been upon the walls long before he had been born.

"You must understand that this is not our primary residence," he said. "It is a country home, one which provides a respite from the larger cities. We have, perhaps, neglected it in the past."

"I believe my great-grandmother spent most of her time here," Faith said, recalling what Cassandra had told her.

"For the short time she was married to my great-grandfather's brother?" he said, a slight, nearly imperceptible edge to his voice.

"Yes," Faith said, her voice firm.

Eric looked over to her with a hint of a smile on his lips, and she wondered just what he thought of her forwardness.

Not that it mattered.

They had just entered the drawing room when *Don*

Raphael stopped, staring straight ahead of him, and then circled, looking around the room.

"Is something amiss?" Faith asked, and he tapped a finger on his chin.

"This painting..." he said, pointing to the landscape of the Bay of Biscay on the wall.

"Yes?"

"It must have been moved here recently."

"Moved?" Faith repeated as she and Eric exchanged a glance. "Does the staff often switch out paintings?"

"Never," he said, shaking his head, then lifted his hands in the air before continuing. "Ah, perhaps I am seeing things."

Faith paused for a moment, tilting her head as she peered at it.

"What is it?" Eric asked her in a low tone.

"I recognize it," she said.

"It's Spanish," he said, scrunching his nose. "How could you have seen it?"

"I could have sworn it was in my bedchamber here. Do you recall?"

His eyes twinkled. "I wasn't looking at the paintings when I was in there."

She swatted him lightly as *Don* Raphael looked back, having either shaken off his confusion or chosen to hide it from them. "Are you lovebirds coming?"

They continued, but Faith couldn't help another look at the painting. There was a rather odd square behind it – as though one of a different shape had been hanging there before.

But *Don* Raphael had continued, and they had no choice but to follow.

"That is all for the house," he said. "Many rooms, many heirlooms, nothing particularly interesting. I am honestly not certain what you would like from your visit here?"

Faith smiled, hoping she appeared as friendly as Cassandra would have.

"I simply wanted a better understanding of my great-grandmother's life," she said, trying to think of a reason why they might want to spend so much time here. "I happened upon some of her journals and I'd like to see them come to life, is all."

For the first time since they had arrived here at the Palencia estate, it seemed that had piqued *Don* Raphael's attention.

"Your great-grandmother wrote journals?"

"Ah... yes," Faith said, looking to Eric for help with her story, and he stepped forward.

"From what my wife says, she was a prolific writer," he said. "Her descriptions were so vivid that Faith had to come to see them for herself."

"I see," *Don* Raphael said, stepping closer. "And just what did she have to say about her family and the estate?"

"Only how beautiful it is here and how much she missed everyone once she moved away."

"I see," he said, an assessing glint in his eyes that was as concerning as the emptiness of the house itself. "Would you like to see the grounds?"

"That would be lovely," Faith said. "The climate here is so temperate."

"That it is," he said. "Although Madrid's weather is equally fine, is it not?"

"Of course," she said in a rush, nearly forgetting that she was not supposed to be from England, where the weather was so much drearier than any place in Spain.

They continued out of doors to the beautiful grounds, and Faith nearly forgot herself and their true purpose for being here as they walked among the lush greenery. A small river ran right through the gardens, and she was tempted to follow it to see where it might lead.

"This way," *Don* Raphael said, taking them up a slight incline. Here the path was less clear, and Faith's skirts caught a couple of times on branches that reached out toward her in an attempt to capture her.

"Where are we going?" Eric asked, holding out an arm that Faith continued to purposefully ignore, needing to prove that she could walk without his aid. She had no wish to become reliant on him, nor for him to believe that she needed him to accomplish anything she was here to do.

"It's a surprise," *Don* Raphael answered, causing Faith to look up, wondering at his tone. Had it turned sinister or had she been listening to Eric more than she should have been? "Up the stairs now."

They had entered a clearing, a stone structure appearing in the middle of it, so fitting to the landscape that it appeared to be part of it. Whoever had built it had certainly had a great interest in keeping it from appearing too ostentatious.

Faith lifted her skirts and started up behind *Don* Raphael, Eric behind her.

"What is this?" Eric asked.

"It is a lookout," *Don* Raphael answered. "To keep an eye out for any approaching ships."

Eric's hand touched her waist as they started up the stairs, and she turned to him with a slight shake of her head, causing him to lift his palm as though in defence and then back away.

Guilt tugged at her, but it was just as important that he understand her independence as she remember who she was and what the two of them meant to one another – a bit of fun. Nothing more. To become too attached would only lead to heartbreak that she had promised herself she would never face again.

So consumed was she by her thoughts and memories that she wasn't paying as much attention as she should to where she was stepping. They had neared the top of the tower when the stone under her foot seemed to crumble beneath her step, and she cycled her arms wildly, searching for purchase.

She thought she had nearly caught herself when she slipped backward, her ankle twisting painfully. She fought for foothold, anything to grasp onto, but it was no use.

She was falling down the stairs – with nothing behind her but stone.

CHAPTER 13

⚜

*E*ric's stomach had twisted the moment *Don* Raphael led them to this structure – and the higher they climbed, the more nervous he had become.

He usually wasn't a man given to nerves, so that was saying something. However, it seemed that when it came to Faith, his usual carefree attitude failed him. He *cared*. Which was concerning in itself.

Then Faith had lost her footing, and time seemed to stand still.

He was a few feet behind her, giving her the space she had asked for with her stare if not her words. Why she was so disinclined to accept any help he had offered her thus far, he had no idea, but it meant that when she began to fall he wasn't immediately behind her – but he had enough time to shift sideways to catch her before any damage was done.

Thank goodness.

He moved quickly behind her, his arms wrapping around her. Her weight fell upon him, and the moment she was in his arms, the world righted itself. He knew then that he would do anything to make sure that no harm ever came to her.

No matter what she believed, she was his responsibility, and he took that seriously.

"Faith? Are you all right?" he asked as she winced in pain.

"My ankle," she said, her voice just above a whisper as she was obviously trying to mask her pain – of course. She wouldn't be Faith if she showed exactly how she was truly feeling. "It twisted, but I do not believe there is any significant damage."

"We'll return you to the house," he said, before looking up at *Don* Raphael, who was watching them without a word, an inscrutable look on his face. "*Don* Raphael, did you know that these stairs were dangerous?"

"Of course not," he said, crossing his arms over his chest. "I would never have led you up here if I had. I only intended to show you the view of the ocean from the lookout."

Eric studied the stair, noting the pieces of rock that had broken upon Faith's step scattered below them. "It is odd that the step would break beneath Faith's weight but not your own."

Don Raphael's eyes narrowed.

"Are you accusing me of something?"

"Simply making an observation," Eric said, attempting to keep his voice light. They were in this man's territory and it would be of no help to anyone if he angered him. "We must return to the house."

He bent, placing one arm under Faith's knees, the other around her back as he lifted her, ignoring her protestations.

"I am fine, Eric," she said, but he shook his head.

"You are not," he said, wanting to check her ankle, but not in front of *Don* Raphael.

Fortunately, they were not far and began the walk back to the house, albeit slowly. When they entered the front door,

Abello was waiting for them, a concerned look across his usually expressionless face.

"What has happened?" he asked and Eric told him as briefly as he could.

"I am going to take Faith upstairs," he said. "If we require further assistance, I will send a request."

At that, he began up the stairs, feeling the weight of her gaze upon him.

"I am sure I can walk," she said. "I must be getting heavy."

"Lucky for you, I spend a great deal of time in athletic pursuits," he said. "Therefore, I have no difficulty. Although…" he couldn't help but tease her, "I must say, you have required a great deal of maintenance in the past few weeks. First, your hand. Now, your ankle… you are such a delicate flower."

She snorted, proving his point. "While I am far from the most graceful woman you have ever met, delicate is likely the last word to ever describe me."

"Is that so?" he said as he walked across the landing and into her chamber, then laid her across the bed.

"That is so," she returned. "Hope is the graceful, delicate one. Unfortunately, she received all of the poise."

"The perfect princess."

"Yes," Faith said, although without any malice. "She most certainly is."

Sensing that this was an area of discomfort for Faith, Eric made himself comfortable beside her on the bed as he slowly pushed her skirts away from her ankle before unlacing the boot she had worn for their tour.

"You know," he said conversationally, "not everyone prefers a princess."

"Of course they do," she insisted. "Hope is everything a man could want."

"Your sister is a lovely woman, true," he noted. "But she does not call to me."

"No?" she said, and he could tell she was holding herself back from asking just who did call to him.

He decided to take pity on her and tell her anyway.

"I like a woman who challenges me. Who has some grit, I suppose you could say. Who can rescue herself – even if it is rather fun to rescue her time and again."

As he finished unlacing her boot, he slid it off her foot and glanced up, finding her lip between her teeth.

"Does that bother you?" he asked. "I know sometimes I speak without thinking, but if you'd prefer not to hear it—"

"It's not that," she said, shaking her head. "It is only that this is not something I am used to hearing. I believe it is hard for men to see me through Hope. I do love her, more than anyone else in this world, but that does not mean that it is easy to stand next to her beauty all the time."

He nodded, sympathetic to what she was saying, even if he had a hard time understanding how anyone could overlook Faith.

"Your ankle is swollen. A bit red and angry," he said, running his fingers over it. "Does it hurt more when I touch it?"

"A bit," she said. "I'll rest it for a while, and hopefully it will improve."

He carefully placed it on a pillow before inspecting it for any further damage, but as far as he could feel, all was well. It would likely heal in due time.

Faith lay back and Eric stretched out next to her, propping his head up with one hand.

"You know," he said, circling a finger around the floral pattern in the covering, "*I* chose you. Two years ago, before Hope was promised to anyone else. I am sure that, had I expressed interest in her, an arrangement could have been made between us. I had the title coming to me, after all."

"My father wanted me to marry first."

"Still, when it came to it, he allowed Hope to marry before you, did he not?" Eric asked. "You, however, are missing my point. I didn't choose her. I chose you. And not for your dowry or your connections. Those are available everywhere you turn on the marriage mart. I chose you for you."

"We never discussed marriage," Faith said. "It was just a kiss."

"It was more than that."

Faith's eyes were hooded, her expression hidden as she watched his finger.

"We do not need to speak of this," she said, her voice just above a whisper.

"I think we do," he said, reaching up and using his forefinger and thumb to lift her chin so that she was looking at him. "Do you know how excited I was? I thought I had finally found a woman who I could spend more than one night with. Who would not bore me. Who had as many answers as she did questions. Who yearned for more in life than a title. Our conversations on the dance floor, or in the gardens, they meant something to me. As did our kiss."

"That was my first kiss," she said quietly. "But it certainly wasn't yours."

Her comment took him aback. He hadn't thought that mattered to her, but it appeared he was wrong.

"No," he agreed. "It was not."

"Our conversations meant something to me too," she said. "And our kiss was... everything. It was *everything* to me. But I know it meant nothing to you."

"How can you say that?" he asked, both truly curious as well as slightly annoyed that she would assume such things about him. "You have no idea what I was thinking. And that night, the night that I thought was the start of, well, the start of a life together, you just left, like—"

"Like I saw you kissing another woman?" Her head snapped up as she was no longer hiding her emotion, but allowing him to see the anger that was written upon it – anger, and pain.

He opened and closed his mouth as he tried to find the correct response.

"That wasn't what it looked like—" he attempted, but she wasn't listening.

"I came back to find you," she continued, bitterness dripping off her every word. "There you were, hidden in an alcove, kissing another, as though nothing had happened between you and me."

Eric rubbed his temple as he remembered the details of that night. The encounter had been so brief in a place so obscured that it had never occurred to him that they could have been seen. But of course they had. By the one person who mattered the most.

"I thought she was you," he explained, staring at her imploringly, wishing she would believe him. "I had closed my eyes, if the truth be told, and found that spot in the alcove to sleep off some of the drink. When I felt lips on mine, in my dreams, I assumed you had returned. I told the woman to leave me alone, but you must have missed that part. I had no idea you saw it."

He met her eyes, finding that she was blinking tears away, but he said nothing when she hid her face.

"That is quite the story," she finally said.

"It is the truth," he said with a shrug. "Believe it if you wish. Or don't. But know that I am not one to lie – especially to you. Faith, the way I feel about you is never going to change. I will also not, however, spend the rest of my life trying to prove to you that I am a better man than you believe me to be. If you cannot accept my truth, then so be it. Once we return to England, you go your way and I will go mine."

He knew that his words might be harsh – and they killed him to say – but she had to understand his perspective.

"This is about your pride, then?" she said in a gutted voice.

"Call it what you want," he said, pushing himself up and off the bed, surprised by his response to her lack of trust in him, "but that is my truth. I am a powerful man, it seems, in every way but when it comes to you."

She stayed where she was, lying on the bed, her eyes averted from him. He longed to kiss away the tension on her forehead, to heal all of her wounds, both the physical ones and those inside of her, but he knew that he had done what he could. All that was left now was to wait. Wait for her to recognize her worth, and to realize that he was the man who would always respect it.

He just wasn't sure how long it would be until his patience wore out.

CHAPTER 14

Faith was miserable.

Part of it was that her ankle was causing not only pain but also inhibiting her from moving about and accomplishing what they had come here to do.

The other part was realizing that Eric spoke so much truth.

She wasn't sure if he actually cared about her as much as he purported to or whether he was simply speaking sweet words to her to try to return to her bed. But he was correct in that she didn't quite trust that he could actually want her because he enjoyed her company. She knew she could be prickly, unwilling to show anyone what she was truly thinking – for she was too afraid of what they might think of her in turn.

This was all quite convoluted, especially as the two of them were currently posing as husband and wife. But not tonight. Tonight, she would stay in her own chamber and he within his.

They hadn't needed to speak about it. She had understood from their conversation that she had to be the one to open the door – literally and figuratively – and take the next step. She just wasn't sure how far that journey would take them.

Now, they could take their time and do as they pleased. Once they returned to England, however? That was another story altogether. They could continue this relationship or not, but they would never have this time alone together again without the presumption of a serious courtship that could only have one conclusion. A conclusion that caused her an apprehensive excitement that scared her.

This was why she never should have kissed him. It complicated the relationship between them and distracted them from their true mission. They hadn't even discussed the treasure or finding the next clue since they had taken the ill-advised step forward together.

Faith knew her ankle would heal if she kept it immobile, so as much as she hated remaining affixed to her bed, she hoped doing so would allow her to walk upon it by morning.

Despite how tired she was, she slept fitfully, until sometime in the early hours of the morning she came completely awake. She blinked her eyes, surprised to find it still dark, wondering why she had awoken so suddenly until the sound of scrapes and scuffles had every part of her on edge.

She lifted her head ever so slowly to look about the room, but only blackness and a few shapes were visible. Nothing amiss that she could see. But it wasn't what she could *see*—it was what she could hear.

Someone was in her room. She was sure of it.

She stayed as still as she could, barely breathing as she didn't want the intruder to notice that she had awoken. It couldn't be Eric – he wasn't the type to tiptoe anywhere. If he had wanted to return to her bedroom, he would have done so by throwing the door open with a loud exclamation before pouncing on her bed.

"Where is it?" she heard a muffled voice say as the doors of the wardrobe squeaked open. A thud resounded before a curse, and just as Faith was deciding whether to confront the man or allow him to finish his search and leave without confrontation, the door to Eric's bedroom opened with a loud creak.

"Faith, why are you out of bed?" he mumbled, rubbing the slumber from his eyes, and then in a flurry of motion, the figure in her wardrobe leapt across the room to the door. Eric took a second too long to note the additional presence, and before he had the wherewithal to realize that it wasn't Faith prowling about the room, the door was open and the man escaping.

"You, there! Stop!" Eric called out, pursuing the figure out the door, and Faith sat up, wishing she could chase after them but knowing that she would do nothing but impede Eric's progress, especially with her injured ankle.

She waited tensely until quick returning footsteps sounded outside her door, the soft padding reassuring her that they belonged to Eric.

"Faith?" he said, pushing the door open before closing it behind him. "Are you unharmed?"

"I am," she said as Eric lit the candle on the side table before sitting on the edge of her bed. Despite the tense conversation between them earlier, he reached out and covered one of her hands with his, and she appreciated the comfort. "I awoke to the sound of him rustling about my room but stayed still. I was deciding whether or not to confront him when you appeared."

"I wasn't able to sleep and heard noises," he said. "I thought it was you up and about on that ankle."

"So you came to send me back to bed?" she asked wryly.

"I came to see that all was well," he said softly. "And it is a good thing I did."

Faith sobered, allowing her ire to fade away, knowing that Eric spoke the truth. "Did you catch him? Did you see who it was?"

"No," he said, shaking his head. "By the time I began my chase, he had disappeared. To where, I have no idea. The other bedrooms are locked, and there is no other way out besides the staircase, but I didn't hear his tread upon the steps. The only other escape would have been over the banister."

"Which would be impossible."

"Yes," he agreed. "It is as though he vanished into the night."

"Must be one of those ghosts you kept going on about," she teased and he wagged a finger at her.

"You joke about that, but one never knows. Could have been."

"Ghosts do not hit their heads on wardrobe shelves and then mutter curse words," she retorted, and he shrugged.

"Depends on the ghost."

She couldn't help but roll her eyes, and he fell back on the bed beside her, closing his eyes as his exhaustion took over.

"We do have one problem," Faith said, wincing as she knew it was likely the last thing he wanted to hear but it must be said.

"Which is?"

"He heard you enter my chamber speaking English to me. English without a Spanish accent. Whoever was here will now be suspicious that we are not who we say we are."

"It is not as though anyone can admit that they were spying on us by sneaking into your chamber."

"No," she said, "but we are on their home soil, which is a great disadvantage for us."

"What do you suggest we do now?" he asked.

"We must solve this clue or find this treasure quickly and

depart as soon as possible," she said. "Otherwise, I fear we could be in danger."

"I wish you had never come to Spain," he muttered, causing Faith's heart to drop, bitterness spreading through her veins like poison. She hated how much she allowed his words to affect her, for it showed just how much she cared.

"I apologize that you have to spend so much time with me," she said tersely. "Here I thought you might enjoy it."

"I *do* enjoy my time with you," he said, pushing himself back up to a sitting position as his jaw tightened. "If you do not know that by now, then you do not understand me at all. It is more important to me, however, that you are alive and well than having a good time with me."

"Is that not your main concern? Having a good time?"

He muttered something indiscernible before standing from the bed and walking back toward his room, bumping into furniture as he went. Faith's breath hitched, and she called his name softly.

"Eric?"

He stopped, though he didn't turn back around, his broad frame tense beneath the nightshirt that was draped around him.

"I am sorry," she said, dipping her head. "I should never have said that. I just… I am afraid to let anyone too close, and I do not always consider that there is more behind the words than how they sound. The truth is…"

"The truth is you are scared. Scared that you might be hurt."

She nodded, wishing she could lift the blanket and scurry beneath it to hide from his stare, but knowing that hiding was what had gotten her to this point.

He sighed as he turned, running a hand through his long, dark hair. "I hate that I am the one who caused you to feel such a way."

"If it makes you feel any better, I was never a very nice person to start with," she said with a humorless laugh.

"You have kindness within you," he said. "You just do not allow many people to see it."

She didn't have much of a response to that. All she knew was that she enjoyed his company more than she would ever like to admit, and she didn't want him to leave – not tonight, not when they returned to England, not forever.

But had she ruined everything?

"What do we do now?" she asked.

"Now, we find the clue and get the hell out of this place." He winced. "Probably shouldn't have said that."

Faith laughed. "I think we are well past the point of tempering our words around one another. Besides, as we have established, I am not exactly a delicate young lady. I am beyond the age that I can be considered a young lady. Old spinster is more like it."

"If you are an old spinster, what does that make me?" he asked, lifting a brow. "I believe I have a year or two on you."

"Which is allowed for men," she said wryly. "It is hardly fair. But, Eric?"

"Yes?"

"When I asked you where we go from here, I was not just referring to our actions regarding the treasure and our travel."

"I know," he said, taking a seat on the bed once more, except this time at the foot of it, farther from her. "I suppose we have gone about all of this the wrong way. We have taken twists and turns and done things all out of order."

"So…"

"So why do we not start at the beginning?" he asked, his signature grin returning. "Pleasure to meet you. I am Lord Ferrington."

She looked at him dubiously, just able to make out his

shape with the moonlight through the window. "You do know we are still sitting in my bedchamber."

"You are no young lady, however, so does it matter?" he asked with an expression that she knew was meant to challenge her. "So, tell me, who might you be?"

She decided it was best to play along.

"It is a pleasure to meet you, Lord Ferrington. I am Lady Faith, but you may call me Faith if you wish."

"That is very forward of you," he said with a wink.

"Some might say that I am too forward a woman," she said. "But someday, a man will come along who appreciates that."

"What a lucky man he will be," he said. "You may call me Eric if we are going to be on such familiar terms."

"Very well, Eric," she said. "I do hope we can be good friends."

"I would like that," he said. "Perhaps we could spend more time together."

"That sounds agreeable."

"Tomorrow?"

"Tomorrow it is."

He took her hand in his, lifting it until he pressed the back of it against his lips.

Somehow, the gesture was nearly as sensual as anything they had ever done together before.

It was a new start. And she was looking forward to the next chapter.

CHAPTER 15

*E*ric missed having Faith in his bed.

What surprised him was that what he missed the most was simply her presence. Her lemony scent wafting over him. Her soft touch on his face. Her hair tickling his nose. Her cheek pressed against his chest in the morning.

But he had promised himself that this time, they would go slow. They would do this right, come to know one another and, in the process, he would teach Faith that she was worth loving. As long as she was willing to take the steps to trust him.

He had, however, slept lightly and with the door between them open to ensure that she didn't receive any more unwanted visitors overnight.

A chill crept over him at the thought of her alone with someone in the room. He was still slightly shivering from it when he walked through their connecting door the next morning.

"Good morning," he said cheerfully, finding her face down in her bed, the blankets pulled up over her head. For as productive a woman she was, she was not particularly pleasant first thing in the morning.

"Mpphf," came the noise from beneath the pillow as he sank down on the bed next to her, rubbing her back to gradually wake her.

"Today is the day we are going to find our clue," he said confidently. "Then back to England, we shall go."

She flung her arms up before stretching her entire body from top to bottom, and Eric had to look away so he didn't focus on the way her nightgown strained over her bottom.

Slow, he reminded himself. Instead, he stared at the wall across from the bed, his eyes trained on the painting. Or was it a painting? It looked more like a map. An oddly shaped map.

He stood, walking over to it as he studied it with his hands in his pockets.

"Faith?"

"Mmmhhmm?"

"Has this always been here?" he asked, lifting a hand out of his pocket and pointing to it.

He heard a sigh that he assumed meant she was finally awakening despite her desire not to, and she leaned forward, peering at it.

"Actually… no."

It seemed that this was what would finally get her out of bed.

She walked over to the wall, her nightgown trailing along the floor behind her.

"Do you recall the painting that *Don* Raphael was confused about?" she asked, recognition lighting in her eyes.

"I do."

"*That* was why it looked so familiar – it was the painting that had been on this wall since we arrived. It was replaced. With this."

"But why?" he asked. "Who would do that if it wasn't *Don* Raphael? And what is this?"

"I wish I had answers, but I am afraid I only have the same questions as you," she said. "As for what it is, it looks almost like a map, but of no place that I recognize. Do you think it could be somewhere nearby? There are no hills, though. And it doesn't look like the Bay, although it does appear to be a body of water."

"Do you think this is what the intruder last night was looking for?"

"No." She shook her head. "Whoever was here last night was looking in my belongings. I am sure of it."

He lifted his head toward her. "Did you tell *Don* Raphael about anything of note that you had brought with you?"

She rubbed her eyes, and he could tell she was trying to clear the fog.

"I do not think so… wait!" she stopped, turning to him with wide eyes. "The journals."

"Journals?"

"I told him that my great-grandmother had written in journals. Perhaps that was what he was looking for."

"Ah, that's right. If he is looking for the same treasure that we are, perhaps he thinks that these fictional journals contain a clue."

"And if it was *Don* Raphael that was in my room last night, now he knows that we might not be who we say we are."

"We need to solve this."

"How?"

"I have the necklace piece," Eric said, holding up a finger. "Stay here."

"Where else would I go?" she asked with a laugh, but he ignored her as he was already moving to his room, searching

THE LORD'S COMPASS

through his belongings until he found what he was looking for – the small piece of the necklace.

He returned, holding it up to the map, sensing Faith walking over to him, looking over his shoulder.

"You're breathing on me," he said, shivering, and she stepped back.

"Sorry," she said. "I'm just excited."

"Here," he said, holding it out to her. "You look first."

"Are you sure?" she said with some hesitation, although she took the piece from his palm.

"Very."

She lifted the necklace piece in front of the painting, peering through it to determine what exactly might be in front of her. Eric watched with eager anticipation, willing his patience to persevere.

At that moment, the sun rose high enough to shine through the window, its light catching the stone within the necklace piece and reflecting off of it to glimmer around the room.

"That's it," he breathed. "Bring it closer to your face."

"Like this?" she asked, holding it to her eye.

"Yes," he said, wishing he could look through with her. "What do you see?"

Eric had to stop himself from nearly jumping up and down as she paused, and then when she finally turned to him, holding the piece out toward him, she wore a large grin on her face.

"Look for yourself," she said.

When he did, he was taken aback by what lay before him.

"It's Castleton," he said, leaning back, his mouth dropping open.

"It has to be," she agreed.

He replaced his eye, shifting the piece slightly. It changed the colors of the painting which was, in actuality, a map, as the glass added layers of texture to the painting, showing the topography as well as Castleton itself upon it.

"This piece from the necklace..." he said, holding it up in front of him in awe, "it is more than a clue. It is an instrument that changes everything and... I think it might be a compass."

"A compass?"

"Yes," he said, turning it one way and then the next to better inspect it. "It must be. I think, Faith, if we return to Castleton with it, it will show us exactly where we need to go to find the next clue – or even the treasure itself."

"How could this have found its way here, to Spain?" Faith asked, to which Eric shrugged.

"We will have to ask Ashford and his sister. Perhaps they have more knowledge than we do about their great-grandmother."

"If only there actually were journals," Faith lamented. "Then we might have a better understanding."

"Speaking of that," Eric said. "You better pack. It is time to go home."

* * *

FAITH HAD NEARLY FINISHED PREPARING her bags when there was an urgent knock on her door – and not the door that connected her to Eric.

"Si?" she called out before the door opened, and she jolted in surprise when Abello walked into the room, shutting the door behind him rather furtively for a man of his size.

"Lady Faith," he said in English, "you must go. Now."

Eric must have heard his voice for he was soon striding in from the other room.

"Abello?" he said, his brow furrowed as he looked from

Faith to Abello and back again. "Were you our midnight visitor?"

"Midnight visitor?" Abello repeated, continuing in English as he shook his head. "No. But that would explain everything."

"Explain what?" Faith said, her heart pounding fast as they had obviously been found out. "And why did you call me Lady Faith? And are speaking to us in English?"

"We do not have time to discuss that now," he said in his heavily accented speech. "You must leave before *Don* Raphael returns."

"Where did he go?"

Abello was already crossing the room, removing the map from the wall. He threw it face down on the bed, removing it from its frame as Faith and Eric watched with mouths open in surprise.

"He went to find soldiers to come and arrest the two of you as English spies."

Faith gasped as Eric placed his hands on his hips.

"You cannot be serious."

"I am, unfortunately, very serious. You must be gone by the time he returns."

"But how—"

"He knows you are English and not who you say you are. He must have found something, heard something, I don't know. Did you find the clue you were looking for?"

Faith and Eric exchanged a look, both uncertain of what to say, but Abello continued.

"There is nothing to hide from me. I know about the treasure and received word from England as to who you are and why you are here. You cannot allow *Don* Raphael's family to find it."

"But why?"

"It was not his to begin with, and they will not do the

good with it that your friends will. Now, take the map and return to England. Give it to Mariana's relatives."

"Mariana?" Eric repeated. "You know who Mariana is?"

"Of course. My great-grandfather served her, and those who moved in after her. He passed down the legacy with each generation."

"What legacy?" Faith asked. "I know Cassandra will have so many questions. If you could just tell us—"

She was cut off by a banging and shouts from below, and Abello rolled up the map and passed it to Eric.

"There is no more time," he said. "Come, I will show you a way out."

Eric grabbed their bags as Abello opened the door and looked from left to right. Already, they could hear men below, calling out their assumed identities.

"There is no escape," Eric said, turning from one way to the other in search of an exit as he rubbed his brow in distress. "The stairs will lead us right to them."

"Not these," Abello said, sliding around a statue with surprising agility, into the cutout in the wall behind it. He placed his hand on the statue's head, and just when Faith thought he was going to break it off, it snapped backward, causing the stone wall behind it to groan as it opened the other way.

"A passageway!" Eric exclaimed. "That must be how *Don* Raphael escaped me last night."

"Likely, yes," Abello said, leading them down the stairs beyond. "He also knows about this passageway so it will only give us a few extra moments until he discovers that you are gone."

The entry closed behind them as they rushed down the stairs after Abello. Faith had no choice but to hold onto Eric's arm as she grasped her skirts in the other hand, doing her best not to trip down the stairs on her ankle, which was still sore.

"But what about you?" she asked between pants. "Will he know that you were involved?"

"No," Abello said. "Our family has been loyal servants to the Palencia family for generations. At least, so *Don* Raphael thinks."

At the bottom, the hidden exit led them out into the gardens.

"This is where we part ways," he said. "Follow the river until you are back to the town. Keep hidden, for *Don* Raphael has friends everywhere. You are not safe until you leave San Sebastian."

"Thank you, Abello," Faith said earnestly, as Eric reached out and shook his hand. "I wish you had told us sooner, but thank you for everything."

"I am only playing my role, as you are," he said. "Farewell. And move quickly."

Abello disappeared, returning through the passageway as quickly as he had entered. Faith and Eric looked at one another for a moment in wonderment, their connection broken when they heard a shout.

"They're gone!" resounded from the estate's front entrance.

Eric, carrying both bags, gripped Faith's arm as they took off into a run as fast as Faith's skirts and injured ankle would allow.

"I am holding you back," Faith said, panting, and Eric gave her a sideways glance, even as he was barely breathing any heavier than usual.

"Never," he said. "We are in this together."

They weaved through the trees, following the river, until the town appeared in the distance. Faith wondered how they would ever make it to the port without being noticed, but when they emerged onto a street, Eric slowed them down.

"We will only cause a scene by running," he said. "Best to appear that we belong here – but walk quickly now."

She nodded as he slowed his long stride to match her ungainly one as they made for the port.

"What are the chances there is a departing ship?" she asked.

"I will pay for our passage on the next ship out, no matter what it is," he said. "We will go wherever it takes us – as long as it is staying on the Continent or headed toward England – and then we will find our way back."

"Very well."

He looked down at her, surprise in his eyes.

"Do you trust me?"

Her first smile since they'd been scared out of their room that morning lit her face.

"Actually," she said, nearly as surprised as he was, "I do."

CHAPTER 16

Her faith in him bolstered his spirits.

He only hoped that she wouldn't be upset when she realized just what, exactly, his idea was.

"I do not see any ships," she said, peering up and down the port. "What are we going to do? Should we return to the inn? We could—"

"There," he said, pointing down the wharf.

"Where?"

"The merchant ship."

She squinted. "That looks more like a fishing boat to me."

"It might be," he said, thrusting more confidence than he felt into his words.

"How are we going to—"

"It will not be for long," he promised. "Just until the next town."

She sighed. "Very well," she said, waving him forward. "Do as you think is best."

He practically beamed at her before continuing, finding the captain — he supposed one could call the man that, for it was his ship — and exchanging a few words.

"Didn't catch much this morning so returning to the sea," the man said, rubbing his beard as he looked Eric up and down. "No time to take you anywhere."

"I'll pay you double what you would make off your daily haul to take us just as far as Bilibao," Eric promised, and the man quickly agreed.

Faith said nothing until they had found a seat among smelly fishing nets and bait. Faith had her eyes closed and a handkerchief over her nose, although Eric could tell that she was trying not to draw much notice to her response.

"I do not mean to be rude," she hissed toward him, "but this is something else. What if we do not make it to the next town? We would be lost along with the treasure map. And then what? It would all be for nothing."

"That is what you are concerned about? The treasure? Faith, I am sure everyone would be far more concerned about the loss of our lives than that of a treasure."

She shrugged. "Would they, though? This is a legacy. One that Abello's family has held onto for generations. What was he waiting for?"

"He must have been waiting for someone to return, looking for the clue."

"But why us? How did he know who we were? And why didn't he just say something to us instead of going through all the trouble of switching the painting and pointing us in the right direction? And was he trying to scare us away or was that *Don* Raphael?"

Eric sighed. "I wish I knew, Faith. Perhaps Ashford and his sister will. Until then, we keep this clue – and ourselves – safe."

She nodded absently.

"Very well."

The rise and swell of the boat must have rocked her to sleep, for soon enough she was leaning against him, her head resting on his chest. Eric wrapped his arms around her, holding her back against him as he leaned his head forward and nuzzled her hair, which was still sweetly scented.

He had promised to return her home. Now he just had to make sure he followed through, which was no burden. He had been truthful in what he said. Keeping her safe was all that mattered anymore.

He had undertaken this journey for adventure.

Little had he realized the turn it would take.

When the shores of Bilibao appeared on the horizon, Eric's relief at their safe arrival swelled along with hope when he spotted the large English ship in the harbor. A frigate, from what he could tell. If it was headed in the right direction, it just might mean a speedy passage home, before *Don* Raphael and his friends received any indication as to where they had escaped.

"Thank you," he said, paying the fisherman as promised, who smiled and tipped his hat once docked, apparently having considered his wages for the day rescued – and, from the direction he was taking, might spend a few of them at what appeared to be a tavern.

"What now?" Faith asked as Eric held out his arm to help her onto shore, noting that this time she naturally accepted his offer without protest.

"Well, Bilibao seems to be a slightly larger port than San Sebastian. Hopefully, we can find a ship to take us in the right direction. Do you see the frigate over there?"

Her gaze followed his finger. "I assume you mean the square-rigged sailing ship with the guns?"

"That it is," he said, impressed. "How do you know so much about ships?"

"I'm a fast learner," she said wryly. "So do we just walk up and ask for passage on what appears to be a warship?"

"Let us hope that it does not intend on using those guns,

but instead was selected for its speed," he said. "I'll see if I can speak to someone on the crew. "Once I find out more, we can determine how we will approach this. We can go with it as we determine the best path forward."

"You do not want to plan?" she said, her mouth opening slightly and he laughed.

"Of course not. This is far better!"

She shook her head, and he could practically read her thoughts – on what a different approach he would take – in this and almost anything else.

"We work better together," he said, nudging her with his elbow. "You are trusting me, remember?"

"I remember," she said, shaking her head, but it was with a smile. "How do you know so much about warships?"

"My father was an officer."

"Ah, yes, that's right," she said.

Keeping a tight grip on the bag that held the map, which he had promised Faith he would never let out of his sight, he walked down the dock as nonchalantly as he could until he came upon a group of crewmen. He paused a moment, listening to them chattering with one another, discovering with delight that they were speaking English. Eventually one of them spotted him and they stopped, waiting to see what he wanted.

"Apologies for the interruption," he said. "My... wife and I are looking for passage home. I do not suppose that you will be returning to England anytime soon?"

Two of the crewmen who he guessed to be the most senior exchanged a glance before one of them stepped forward.

"That would not be for us to answer," they said, looking Eric up and down, likely trying to reconcile his polished British accent with his rich Spanish attire. "That would be for our captain – and his guest."

"His guest?"

But they would say nothing further, worrying Eric, for it meant that there was likely something out of the ordinary about this ship, which didn't bode well for their chances of passage.

One of the crewmen lifted his chin, pointing behind Eric, and he turned around with interest to see just who this mystery guest might be.

When Eric turned in that direction, however, he spent no time on the man himself, for he was caught by Faith, who had been waiting for him at the end of the dock.

She was close enough that he could read her expression; far enough that he couldn't be by her side as fast as he would like.

She was rooted to the spot, her body frozen, her posture tense. Her cheeks were flushed, her eyes wide, her mouth quivering, as though uncertain whether to lift her lips in happiness or let them fall open in horror. As Eric moved toward her, he passed by a man who he belatedly realized was also standing still, and as he reached Faith's side, he wrapped his arm around her, drawing her close as he turned to stand with her to face their foe as a united pair.

When Faith spoke, her voice wavered just once, before she cleared her throat and allowed strength to fill it instead.

"Father," she said. "What are you doing in Spain?"

* * *

LORD EMBURY LOVED HIS DAUGHTERS, truly he did, of which both Faith and her sister Hope were aware.

He was also not only protective of them, but he had very specific ideas of how they should behave, who they should marry, and what they were to do with their lives.

Faith's father had made it clear that he wished her to

marry, and yet despite introducing her to gentleman after gentleman, none ever suited her – for none had been Eric.

But she hadn't been about to tell her father that. It seemed she might have the opportunity now.

"What am I doing here?" Lord Embury thundered as he closed the distance between them, his footsteps heavy, his mouth nearly hidden by the beard that covered his wide face, but there was no mistaking the furrow of his brow nor the narrowing of his eyes. "What am *I* doing here? What do you think I am doing here? Possibly chasing my daughter across the ocean? My unmarried daughter, the daughter of an earl, who has ruined herself and this family?"

"Father—"

"Do not 'Father' me," he seethed, his teeth set together. "And you—" he pointed to Eric, poking a finger into his chest. "You... you..."

"Father, he had nothing to do with this," Faith said, stepping in front of Eric, who didn't seem to have an answer for the earl. "This was my idea. He did not know that I had accompanied him until it was too late. Why do we not find somewhere quieter to sit down and talk about this?"

Eric cleared his throat and leaned in. "While I understand there is much to discuss, perhaps, if it appears that we have passage to return to England, could we do this on board the ship? There is a chance that we are being pursued."

Lord Embury turned the full weight of his stare upon Eric, who did not seem overly perturbed.

"Are you telling me that my daughter is in danger?" he practically growled.

"Well, yes, actually, I am," Eric said, his voice as even and as cheerful as ever. "Not to worry – we escaped in time, but I think we should leave Spain as soon as we are able since we have what we came for?"

"Dare I ask what could be so important that you would

leave behind all of your responsibilities and my daughter would risk ruin?" Faith's father said, pushing his grey hair back away from his forehead.

"The next clue in our treasure hunt, of course," Eric said with pride, and Faith winced as her father covered his face with his hands.

"Dear God, this treasure hunt is going to be the end of me," he said before turning to face the boat. "Captain! Tell the crew to board. We will leave at once."

A man who was, apparently, the captain, walked forward on the ship, bellowing back.

"We are not prepared!"

"We'll stop somewhere else," her father said, and Faith had to appreciate that, if nothing else, once he set his mind to something there was no stopping him. "We cannot stay here."

Faith followed her father up to the plank of the ship, and when Eric put his arm out to help her, her father batted it away.

"Enough of that now, you fool," he said, helping Faith himself, and she had to stifle her smile at Eric's surprise, although he remained as nonplussed as ever. "What is wrong with your ankle?"

"That will be part of the story," Faith said, to which her father responded with an even darker glare toward Eric.

"There's a cabin for you, Faith," her father muttered once they came on board. "As for you," he said, pointing at Eric once more, "you can sleep with the crew."

"Father," Faith said, stepping forward when Eric's eyebrows rose as she attempted to stop any controversy before it began, "you are aware that Eric is of the same rank as you."

"We both might be earls, but I certainly never took advantage of a young woman," her father said, his hands on his hips.

"And neither did Eric," Faith said in exasperation.

"Well *Eric* does not seem to understand how dire this situation is," her father said mockingly. "I am glad that the two of you are on such friendly terms, Faith."

"And why is that?"

"Because," he said, a smug smile of satisfaction crossing his face, "soon you will also be calling him husband."

CHAPTER 17

*E*ric had been expecting this. What other result could there be when the two of them had taken a journey to the continent together without a chaperone?

He was not opposed but rather pleased about the situation, since he and Faith were getting on so well.

What he wasn't prepared for was the look of horror on Faith's face.

"Father, you cannot be serious," she said, looking from him to Eric and back again.

"Oh, I am very serious," Lord Embury said, crossing his arms over his chest. "Come, Lord Ferrington, we shall sit in my cabin and work out the details as we set sail."

He began to lead them across the deck to the cabin that he had claimed as his own, one which Eric would guess was the most spacious on the ship, when he stopped suddenly and whirled around with rather surprising dexterity for a man of his girth.

"Where do you think you are going?" he asked Faith, who was following along.

"I am accompanying you," she said resolutely. "If my fate

is going to be discussed, then I am going to be there to discuss it."

"This is not how these things work, Faith," her father said, but she crossed her arms and remained rooted to the spot. Eric loved her stoicism.

"I am not my sister," she said. "I know Hope allowed you to make these arrangements, but I will not be sitting outside the door with my ear to the keyhole while you and Eric decide everything. Besides, do you want me to remain out here alone in plain sight for all of the crew members?"

Her father let out a sigh and scrubbed a hand over his face, indicating that Faith had, at least, won this argument.

"Fine," he said through gritted teeth. "But you will just listen to the conversation."

Faith snorted in obvious disagreement but she wisely said nothing until they were within the cabin, seated around the small dining table that was shifting back and forth with the ship as it began its crawl out to sea, although Eric knew that a frigate such as this would quickly pick up speed once it reached the open water.

"So tell me, Father," Faith began, ignoring her instructions not to speak, "how did you know where I was? And why did you travel all this way yourself?"

"One of your mother's acquaintances, Lady Maude, sought out Hope and Whitehall upon her travels to Scotland," he explained. "She wrote to us, and imagine our surprise when we learned that you were nowhere near the pair of them. Being that your sister also ran off not too long ago, I was immediately suspicious. I hired a private investigator to find you. It didn't take long to find someone who could place you on the packet ship to Bilibao."

Eric wondered whether their detour to Bilibao was fortunate or unfortunate.

He knew the packet ship they had sailed upon had been

heading there originally. Eric had convinced the captain to make a stop for them in San Sebastian – for a bit of extra coin.

As unhappy as Lord Embury was now, if they had missed him, he didn't want to think about what could have happened to the Englishman while he was searching for his daughter in Spain.

"As you know, I am well aware of this treasure hunt due to my involvement in the clue that Hope and Whitehall found not long ago," he said, to which they nodded, remembering very well the codes that Lord Whitehall had been asked to break, and the role Lord Embury had to play. In the end, they'd had to share with him the reason behind their work.

"What were you thinking?" Lord Embury asked Faith now, continuing before she had a chance to answer. "How could some treasure be so important that you were willing to risk everything?"

"That's the thing," she said, slowly. "What did I have to risk? My reputation, sure, but I have no wish to marry anyway. So I am a scandal. Since Hope is already married, what does it matter? I wanted to do something that had meaning. To have a bit of adventure, see the world? Is that so bad – if no one ever finds out?"

Eric admired Faith for her words, knowing she was likely realizing the truth as she spoke it. He understood that thirst for adventure, that need for something more. He had everything an Englishman could ever want, and yet he was always chasing after the next dare.

"You know, ever since you and your sister were born, people have always said to me, 'Lord Embury, you poor man, to not have a son,'" Lord Embury said, leaning toward Faith, and Eric found himself ready to stand and defend her, even if she was the man's daughter. "I always told them it didn't matter, that I was blessed with the two most wonderful daughters a man could ever ask for and that was enough for me. Between you and your sister and the actions you have taken in the past few months, however, I am now beginning to wonder if they were right!"

"I assure you, Lord Embury, that they are still the daughters you always thought they were," Eric said, attempting to appease the man, but Lord Embury ignored him.

"I thought I had raised you better. Now, you have no choice but to marry the man you attached yourself to upon these travels," her father said, sitting back in his chair as he finally assessed Eric.

Eric shrugged. It was what he had wanted all along, anyway. True, he would have preferred that Faith came to this decision on her own, but if Eric was going to be forced to marry, he was glad it was to Faith.

"Understandable, Lord Embury," he said.

"Understandable?" Faith said, her mouth opening, her agreement not as ready. "Father, when you first caught Hope with Lord Whitehall in the middle of the night, you said you would forget it ever happened. You didn't allow that to bind their fates until they chose it."

"That is true," he said. "But that was in the study of my home. This is an entirely different situation!"

"Father, you cannot force this."

Eric's stomach twisted at the vehemence in her tone.

"Faith, I thought we were becoming friends, were we not?" he asked.

"A friendship does not make a marriage."

"It could be worse," Eric countered, before leaning over the table toward her father.

"Lord Embury, might I have a minute to speak to Faith about this?"

"Go ahead," he said, sweeping his hand out.

"I was hoping to speak to her alone."

"Alone?"

"Yes."

Her father looked from one of them to the other before sighing once more.

"What difference does it make now, anyway?" he asked, flinging his hands into the air before pushing back his chair, causing it to scrape across the floor before he left the room with heavy footsteps.

"Well?" Faith said, tipping back her chair so that she was able to see him better. "What do you have to say that is supposed to convince me into marriage?"

"Just that, it could be much worse, could it not?" Eric said, hating the bit of vulnerability that crept into his chest. "You and I do get along, now that we have cleared up that little misunderstanding from all those years ago. As far as I am concerned, we are friends, and not only that, but we have a connection. I know I feel a pull toward you. I assume you feel that for me based upon the times we have shared a bed."

Her eyes didn't quite meet his, telling him that he was correct in that.

"Perhaps," she said slowly. "But we are so different from one another. After a time, I am sure that we would have *too many* differences. And besides, I—"

"You what?"

"I do not want to be worried about where you are every evening."

"Well, unless you are opposed to me spending most evenings with you," he said, reaching out and gently placing his fingers beneath her chin so that he could tip her face up to look at him, "then I do not think we will have many issues."

"And what about the other evenings? The ones that you

are out? Will you have a mistress? Or a different flavor of woman each night?"

Eric was affronted by that. "Why would you believe I would be with other women?"

"Because you *enjoy* bedding a variety of women?"

"Perhaps I did in the past," he admitted, knowing he had to be cautious in how he approached this. "But I was only ever with other women because I was not with you."

"Eric," she said, her tone making it obvious she did not believe him. "What could you possibly want with me that would be worth so much to you?"

"Well, there is the fact that you are rather ornery and have very strong opinions," he joked, and she rolled her eyes.

"I thought you were supposed to be convincing me to marry you."

"I am getting to that part," he said. "This is the lead up."

"There is nothing you can say to make me change my mind from the fact that I am better off alone," she said.

"I agree," he returned.

"That I am better off alone?"

"No, that nothing I can say can change your mind."

"What is that supposed to mean?"

"Only that you can still be who you are. I like who you are. But you can be yourself and also have this."

"What do you mean—"

Before she could continue, he leaned forward in his chair, lifted her from hers, and, upon her startled gasp, pulled her against him and took her mouth in a deep, searching kiss. She was clever with her tongue when it came to conversations, but he was equally skilled with his in this.

Her resistance lasted just a couple of seconds, and Eric could feel the shift when she gave in, melting into his touch, his embrace, her body melding flush against his.

"Eric," she murmured against him, and he answered her

by wrapping his arms around her, one hand lacing into her hair so that he could tip her head backward to better search her mouth.

He skillfully drove his tongue in, tasting her, branding her, showing her that she was his, no matter how much she tried to deny it.

Her palms slid up over his chest as she arched her body in toward him, confirming that she wanted this – needed *him* – more than she even realized.

Faith's nipples grew hard against his chest and her breath hitched, her fingertips curling into him despite all of her protests and any attempts to push him away.

"Eric," she moaned again, and while he knew that she was pleading for more, they couldn't go any further, as much as he sorely wanted to. Not here. Not now.

Yet he knew, deep within him, that he had never kissed a woman like this. Had never held a woman in his arms with such a compelling need to keep her there, had never had this desire to convince her to return to him, again and again. For he didn't see how he could ever get enough of her.

She had asked why. Why her? What was different? The answer was a difficult one, for the truth was, *she* was the answer.

"You are perfect," he murmured against her mouth, trying to make her understand that he would never hurt her, that she was exactly what he needed.

He kissed her deeply, expertly, happy about all the women who had come before her because it meant that he could be perfect for her and be everything she needed.

He shifted them backward until she was leaning against the table, her hands behind her to keep herself steady.

They lost themselves in the moment and in one another until the ship rocked at the same time that a knock sounded on the door, and Eric sprang backward when Faith pushed him off of her, as they stood, staring at one another in shock, before the door opened and Faith's father walked in.

He looked from one of them to the other, clearly understanding what had occurred and displeased about it, until Faith opened her mouth, her eyes upon Eric the entire time.

"Very well," she said. "I will marry you."

CHAPTER 18

Faith had allowed her body to think for her.

Unfortunately, that acceptance had been all that her father and Eric had needed to quickly plan a marriage agreement – likely before she could change her mind again. While Faith had insisted on participating in any conversation that pertained to her future, she was certain that more than one had occurred without her knowledge on the short passage home to England. It did not take nearly as long as their journey south, for the frigate her father had hired was built for speed, but it felt much longer as the tensions were high.

Her father was obviously still displeased with how all of this had come about.

And then there was Eric himself.

Try as she might, Faith hadn't been able to forget how it had felt to be in his arms, his lips upon hers.

Her body had betrayed her, wanting him, needing him, would have likely given in and taken more had he allowed it. And it wouldn't forget. It wanted more from him and was as eager for their wedding night as she was resistant of the wedding itself.

They were just a few days away from England when Eric found her standing at the railing, gazing over the ocean stretching before her, a shawl wrapped around her shoulders. Her father was speaking to the captain, close enough that he could keep an eye on her but far enough away that he wouldn't be able to hear their conversation.

Not that it appeared either of them had much to say.

They stood in silence for a few moments, until Eric turned and leaned his hip against the rail as he studied her.

"I can tell you are regretting this agreement," he said as she continued to watch the waves, hopeful to spot a flip of a fin or the jump of a fish so that she could draw attention to it and away from this conversation.

"I am not regretting it," she said carefully. "But I do not like that you tricked me into it."

"I did no such thing," he said, leaning in close, his voice husky and oh, so seductive. "I was only giving you a taste of what married life could be."

"That is what our marriage will be?" she said, lifting a brow. "Enjoying one another in bed and then what, going our separate way for the rest of the day?"

He hesitated. "If that is what you want."

She looked down at her hands. "I haven't decided."

The truth was, if she was going to marry, she would like it to be more than that. She wanted a partner in bed, yes, but also for all of the good times and hard times that would come their way throughout each day. She refused, however, to give away too much of herself, in case he shattered her trust and broke her heart once more.

He would never know how much he had hurt her that night. She had explained to him what she had seen, but she could never let him know what she had felt, how she had wondered whether she would ever be the same woman again.

For it had changed her. She had never been as optimistic and carefree as Hope, but, at one time, she had certainly been less cynical, more trusting.

"Is it worth it?" she found herself asking.

"Is what worth it?"

"My dowry."

"What does your dowry have to do with anything?"

"For you to marry me so readily, you must be getting something substantial out of it."

He stared at her so unblinkingly that it unnerved her.

"You still do not understand it, do you?"

"Understand what?"

He answered with a sigh.

"I've tried, Faith, I truly have, and one day, I hope you will be true to both me and to yourself. But until then, will you promise me one thing?"

"What is that?" she asked warily.

"Be open to whatever may come between us?"

She couldn't deny that there was a large part of her – mostly the feminine places – that was very much looking forward to what was to come between them on their wedding night and beyond. She likely knew more than most innocent young ladies did from the scandalous books she and her friends secretly read, but she had never quite understood the draw.

Until now.

Until Eric.

"Very well," she agreed. "I will be as open as I can be."

She just didn't admit that it was only the physical she would be open to – the rest was too difficult to agree to.

"It has been quite a journey, has it not?" he said, jutting his chin toward the faint stretch of land on the horizon. Since

Faith's father had hired the ship, it would take them to Newfield House, which was on the east coast of England near Harwich.

It was where they would be married.

"It most certainly has," she agreed. "And it is just beginning."

* * *

"Faith I am so, so sorry."

It was a month later and Faith's sister, Hope, was sitting across from her on the canopy bed draped in flowing fabrics, in the room they had shared growing up, despite Newfield Manor having more than enough bedrooms for them each to have had their own.

It was one of the most spacious rooms in the manor, however, adorned with delicate floral patterned wallpaper in soft pastel hues, with tall, carved wooden panels framing the windows, allowing a soft glow of natural light to filter through the heavy damask curtains in shades of rose and gold.

Here, near Harwich, there had been few young women of their age living nearby, and so they had become their own closest of friends.

Even if they were as different as any two sisters could be.

"It is not your fault, Hope," Faith said as she stared at the pale yellow gown laid out on her bed, prepared for the next morning when she and Eric would wed. It was made of the finest silk, with intricate hand embroidery gracing the hemline and the edges of the sleeves, showcasing delicate floral motifs and tiny pearls that her mother had selected. "What are the chances that you would have been seen by someone who would speak with Mother?"

"I should have been more convincing in my lie," Hope

said, far too morose for a woman who had just returned from her honeymoon in Scotland. "Lady Maude asked where you were and I said that you were feeling poorly but then one thing led to another and somehow she ascertained that you were not with us."

Faith crossed the room and took Hope's hands in hers, staring into the luminescent blue eyes that had captivated so many gentlemen. Faith had always known that Hope was the favored one, the beautiful one, the diamond of the first water. She likely would have had a far greater number of marriage proposals had their father not continued to insist that Faith marry first.

"Hope," she said. "It is I who should likely apologize to you. When you had your adventure, I did nothing but chastise you for it and then I did the same."

"Except you, at least, kept my secret."

"I did what I thought was best at the time, and, fortunately, it all worked out," Faith said. "But I should have been more understanding. I can see that now."

"Did you have fun, at least, with Lord Ferrington?" Hope asked, her eyes glistening. "Was it worth it?"

"Oh, Hope," Faith said, the smile she had been hiding behind her fear jumping to her face. "It was dangerous, yes. But it was also exhilarating. I cannot remember the last time that I felt so alive."

"And Lord Ferrington?" Hope persisted, raising an eyebrow. "I was shocked when you undertook this adventure, primarily due to the amount of time it meant that you would be spending with him. Now those few weeks will turn into a lifetime. Did you, at least, enjoy your time with him when you were there?"

Faith felt the warmth stealing up her face, and she tried to turn away toward the window before Hope saw it, but she was too late.

"Oh, Faith," Hope said knowingly. "You *did* enjoy time with him."

Faith's breath hitched. "Perhaps there were… a couple of moments," she said slowly. "He causes me to feel things that I never thought possible. Were they ill-advised moments of weakness? Probably. Did I enjoy them? Yes."

"Faith," Hope said, rising from the bed and walking toward her, taking her hands in hers. "You are allowed moments of joy, moments of happiness. There is no need to feel any shame in them."

"I am not ashamed," Faith said, dropping her hands. "I am terrified."

"Of what?"

"Of enjoying it too much. Enjoying *him* too much. Becoming attached."

"Faith," Hope said cautiously, as though concerned that she was going to scare her, "you do know that you will be married to him, do you not?"

"Of course I do," Faith said. "But that doesn't mean that he is going to be true to me or committed to me and only me."

"Is that what he said?"

"No," Faith said. "Quite the opposite. But he told me once before that he was the man for me, and I believed him. In the end, I was not enough."

"Faith," Hope said, "coming from someone who has known you your entire life, who is closer to you than likely anyone in the world, I implore you to let down that guard. If he gives you any reason to doubt him, then so be it. But until then, perhaps you could find a little happiness."

Faith eyed her sister. "As you have found?"

"Oh, Faith, I could never have thought marriage would be so wonderful," Hope said with a sigh, and Faith couldn't help the happiness that jumped in her heart for her sister.

And this time, that happiness was unaccompanied.

Absent was the pain she had felt – pain of the separation from her sister, pain at the thought of being alone.

While she was getting married, it was not as though she was gaining a true partner – was she?

"I still have trouble understanding how you could find so much happiness with a man as surly as Whitehall, but I am glad of it," Faith said, squeezing her hands.

"If you find even half of that with Lord Ferrington, I will be ever so pleased," Hope said with a wistful smile. "Has Percy arrived?"

"I am here!" They both turned to the trill at the doorway, seeing Faith's closest friend, the former Lady Percy and now Mrs. Rowley, standing within it, dressed, as always, in the latest, most vibrant of fashions, a sapphire blue dress flowing over her curves, a gold sash tied around her waist.

"Percy," Faith said, not only allowing her embrace but actually returning it despite her usual resistance to such a gesture. "It is so good to see you!"

Percy stepped backward, holding Faith out at arm's length as though to inspect her. "Who are you and where is my closest friend, Lady Faith Newfield?" she asked with a smile. "For someone has told me this very intriguing rumor that you are to become my sister-in-law."

"That is correct."

"And this is the same woman who vowed to never again be alone with Lord Ferrington, let alone wed to him? Who chastised everyone else for not being proper enough and then took off on an adventure of her own – across to the continent, no less?"

Faith groaned as she threw a hand over her eyes before dropping down on the bed.

"Sit," she said with a sigh. "What you say is true. I will tell you all. Hope, you are going to have to hear it again."

"I am more than happy to," Hope said, flouncing down

and placing her head on her hand. "And I am sure that Percy would love to hear about the secrets the necklace had hidden."

"Oh, do tell," Percy said, obviously greatly intrigued as she and her now husband – Eric's brother – had been the ones to find it. "But *after* you tell us more about you and Lord Ferrington."

So Faith did, forgetting – for just a moment – what was awaiting her the next day.

CHAPTER 19

*E*ric had imagined this moment many times.

He knew that dreams of weddings were supposed to be for women, and that, as a man, he should be most concerned that he was adhering to his responsibility and taking one step closer to continuing his family line.

But as soon as he had met Faith a few years ago, he had dreamt of her, in this moment, walking toward him in all of her finery, prepared to become his wife.

He had just thought she would be a little happier about it.

He wasn't thrilled with the terror that covered her face as she walked toward him, up the aisle of the small chapel at Newfield. The shimmering fabric clung to her high-waisted bodice, her gentle scoop neckline modest with the lace which covered it. She was almost ethereal with a sheer muslin veil pinned to the soft curls piled on her head.

After she reached him and he shook her father's hand, he decided that as much as he had waited for this moment, had longed for it even, he was not marrying an unwilling woman.

"Faith," he said, leaning in and whispering in her ear, despite the scoff of disapproval from the vicar in front of them, "I am not kidnapping you. If you do not want this, then do not marry me."

She turned wide, shocked eyes upon him. "There would be a scandal."

"So there would," he murmured. "But I would prefer that to a life of misery. I want this. I want you. It is your choice now."

She nodded nearly imperceptibly and he held his breath. He knew that giving her a choice was a gamble, knew that there was a very good chance she would run away and never look back.

Which was why his shoulders sagged in relief and the breath he hadn't even realized he was holding flew out when she turned toward the vicar and gave an affirmative nod to begin. She was accepting this marriage – accepting him.

Eric reached out and squeezed her hand, although he had to drop it when the vicar cast critical eyes down upon them.

Eric released her, but not before a thrill ran through him that she was not only going to be his, but she had agreed to it. Had chosen it.

The weight of his mother's stare pressed into his back, reminding him of her question when he had announced his bride to her – was she the right one? Was she ready for the responsibilities that came with the life of a countess?

He had bristled at first until he had considered that his mother had always been a nearly equal partner to his father, who had spent so much of his time away at war. After his father's death, his mother had put aside her grief to seamlessly maintain her role as countess, even if it was as the mother of the earl this time.

She was wondering if Faith was up to the same task.

Eric had been able to assure her beyond a shadow of a doubt that he had no worries in that regard. Faith was an anchor, unwavering in her strength.

Which she was proving today as she stood there in front of his mother, his brother Noah and his wife, Percy, her parents, her sister, and Lord Whitehall.

Her father had declined the idea of inviting additional guests in fear that word of the events causing this wedding would be too widely shared.

To Eric, none of that mattered. All that mattered was the woman beside him.

They repeated after the vicar, putting into words the sacred oaths that bound them together in marriage, committing their lives to one another.

It was the ultimate step in trust, he supposed. He added a vow to himself that he would allow this marriage to be at her speed, on her terms.

Even if waiting for her to catch up nearly killed him.

* * *

THE WEDDING BREAKFAST was downright awkward.

Faith wished that the rest of their friends could have joined them, but her father had been resolute.

She knew better than to push the issue, for it would only cause additional discontent after he had just overcome his displeasure at her deceitful journey to Spain.

Faith considered that she was old enough now that she didn't need to tell her parents of her every movement.

She had been wrong.

"Now, Lady Ferrington," her mother began, speaking to Eric's mother. "Oh goodness," she said, stopping. "I suppose, Faith, that *you* are now Lady Ferrington, are you not? I will never call you that, of course, so do not fear, Lady Ferrington – the other Lady Ferrington – I will not refer to you as the dowager but as Lady Ferrington, if you are fine with that?

Anyway, tell me, where are you going to live now that Faith will be the lady of the house?"

Faith had to hide her smile behind her hand at Eric's mother's quick blinking in response to her own mother's rapid outpouring of words. It was difficult to keep up with her conversation even if one was accustomed to it. Their mothers had met before, of course, but they were not particularly close.

Faith's eyes flicked over to Hope's husband, Lord Whitehall, who she knew still had to take time to himself to recover after an evening spent with her mother.

"Where will I *live*?" Eric's mother repeated. "Why, I will live in my home, where I have always lived."

"But will not Faith be the woman of the house now?"

Faith wasn't quite as amused anymore.

"She will be the countess, yes," Lady Ferrington said slowly, her fingers tightly encircling the glass in front of her, the only outward sign of her annoyance. "However, I will be there to help ease her into the role, of course."

"Do you have a dower house?" Faith's mother persisted. Faith would have stopped her, but she was rather interested in hearing the answer to this. It was not that she didn't like Eric's mother – goodness, she had just basically met the woman – but she appeared rather as strong-willed as Faith was herself. It could certainly make for an interesting relationship.

It was also a reminder that they had fallen into this without considering what it would mean or what would happen once they were married.

"There is a dower house, yes," Lady Ferrington said with a tight smile. "I am sure that, one day, I will live there."

"What does one day mean?" her mother asked. "Tomorrow or years down the road?"

"Mother—" Faith began to interject, but Eric's mother

held out her palm to stop her, sending a small smile of thanks her way.

"I do not believe that is a point that must be discussed on my son's wedding day," Lady Ferrington said, folding her hands over one another in front of her in a clear indication that she was no longer interested in this conversation. "Tell me, Lady Embury, just what are you going to do now that your daughters are both married and you will be here in this house alone, as you have no sons to call your own?"

Faith exchanged a concerned glance with Eric. As far as she knew, their mothers were on friendly terms even if they were not rather close acquaintances. But it seemed her mother had pushed things too far.

"Lord Embury," Eric said, standing, "I would like to thank you for your gracious welcome to your home, and for your trust in me to look after your daughter."

Lord Embury eyed him with disdain. "Did I have a choice?"

"Father..." Faith said, not liking where this was going.

This wedding was supposed to bring them together, not tear them apart. When Eric had asked her if she was sure she wanted to go ahead, nearly half of her wanted to turn around and run out of that little chapel.

But the side of her that told her to stay just edged out the other. Part of it was because there was no escaping this – her father would make sure of it – but the other part was because, deep within, she *wanted* to be married to Eric.

As much as she had tried to deny it.

"Father," she said, attempting to halt this argument before it began. "We are grateful to be here together today. This is an advantageous match for all of us. You were not so keen on Lord Whitehall at the beginning, and now look how much you approve of him and enjoy his company."

She gestured to the viscount, who grunted in response.

Faith had to prevent herself from rolling her eyes as once again she wondered how her sister put up with him.

Eric leaned in toward her, placing a warm, strong hand on her thigh. There were layers of fabric between them and yet Faith could have sworn that his hand was against her bare skin, searing it with its heat.

"Perhaps the ladies should retire," Lord Embury said to his wife, who nodded.

"Very well," she said with a sigh, before leading the ladies out of the dining room and into the drawing room. It was odd to do so in the middle of the day, made even more so when Faith was wondering what she was supposed to do with Eric once they had time alone together. Faith wondered just when, exactly, would that be?

Ever since they had arrived at Newfield Manor, they had not spent a great deal of time together, as they were never allowed to be alone, and there was nothing she particularly wanted to speak to him about in front of her parents. She had wondered if she should have sent him on to Castleton with the compass and the map so that Gideon could begin his search, but she was concerned that he wouldn't have returned in time for the wedding.

And what if he had never returned at all, but instead took the opportunity to escape from marriage to her? Even though she was not particularly excited about being married, the thought of his rejection of her was nearly worse.

"Percy," she said, coming to her friend's side and lacing her arm through hers, "I must talk to you."

"Is this about the treasure?" Percy said excitedly. "I have been receiving letters from Cassandra, so I do hope that one of us can go and update her first. Whoever does should ensure she has the map and the compass so that Cassandra and her brother can start trying to find the treasure on their land. Can you believe it? After all these years, it looks like the treasure is at Castleton itself? Not only that but through this entire hunt, we were so close and yet it took us so far."

"It *is* hard to believe," Faith agreed. "I hope to travel to see them shortly after the wedding. We are to return to Rowley House soon and then we will continue to Castleton shortly after. Cassandra is to have the baby any day, so we will wait until a time when she can travel to Castleton herself to meet us there, as I know she would not want us – or her brother – searching for the treasure without her."

"Except that I am sure if Lord Ashford knew we were so close, he would insist that we come with the clue."

"I shall talk to Eric about it," Faith said, pausing when she saw both Hope and Percy staring at her.

"What is it?"

Her friend and her sister exchanged a look.

"It is just…" Hope began, "I have never heard you say that you are going to seek out anyone's opinion besides your own."

"That is not true."

They both looked at her skeptically until the gentlemen walked in, taking seats around the room. While they were welcomed by the women, none of them appeared very content.

The conversation was so stilted, so filled with tension, that Faith finally decided she had to put a stop to it.

"I feel slightly unwell," she said, standing from the sofa. Eric immediately stood with her, causing her to feel guilty by the amount of concern that filled his face. "I believe I must go upstairs. Thank you all for coming – especially all of you for travelling such a way. I am so glad that you were able to be here with us."

With that, she swept out of the room.

She hoped that Eric wouldn't follow her but would allow

her to go alone. She needed both time and space to clear her head.

She ran upstairs, calling her maid to help her change into a riding skirt and bonnet as fast as she was able.

If anyone discovered her, they would not understand where she was going or why she had chosen to leave the wedding party – and her husband – behind.

But here she was, walking into the forest on the day that she should have been celebrating. She found the targets where they had been left and notched an arrow into her bow before letting it fly, landing it perfectly within the arch. Every arrow. Every shot. Her practice was paying off. If only she could join any war effort herself, she knew she could do a great deal to help the army.

She heard him come up behind her before she saw him. As quiet as he tried to be, the tread of his step and the heaviness of his breath gave him away.

"I thought I'd find you out here," he said, keeping his distance behind her as she lifted the bow and pulled it back at eye level.

"Why did you need me?" she asked.

"Must I have a reason for wanting to see my wife?"

"That will take some getting used to," she said, releasing the bow and allowing the arrow to fly in a graceful arc before it notched itself into the target with a *thwack*.

"Me wanting to see you?"

Yes. And her constant worry that one day he would stop.

"Being called your wife," was what she said instead.

"It will become more familiar in time," he said.

"You did not need to follow me," she said. "I am not actually ill."

"Obviously," he said. "Do you ever get ill?"

She eyed him from over her bow before notching another arrow.

"Of course I do."

"You seem so strong, it is hard to believe that you are not invincible."

"A misconception, I assure you."

He paused for a moment, his hands in his pockets. "I know you came out here to escape everyone, and I do not blame you. I shall go entertain our guests."

Guilt dropped into her stomach, and she lowered her bow. "I apologize. I never considered that my leaving would mean that you had to take on that responsibility."

He shrugged before winking at her. "That is one responsibility that I do not mind at all. When you need me, you know where to find me."

And at that, he turned around, walking back toward Newfield.

Faith watched him go with a smile on her face. When he stopped, looked one way and then the other as though he had no idea which way to go, she couldn't help it.

She laughed out loud.

This man was something else.

Something else, indeed.

CHAPTER 20

Eric paced in front of the fireplace of his bedchamber.

A bedchamber that was conveniently located next to Faith's. Of course, the two of them had been provided this suite together for their wedding night, but he saw no evidence of her moving into the room.

Which he was fine with. This marriage would go at her pace, he reminded himself.

It still didn't tell him just what he should do – go to bed or wait to see if she might appear. Should he go say goodnight?

Goodness, he had not been this nervous about a woman in years.

His friends had retired for the night, his valet had come and gone, and he hadn't been able to make eye contact with Lord Embury all evening, despite knowing there was little chance that anything would happen between him and Faith tonight.

She had made it abundantly clear that she preferred her

independence and had only married him because she had no other choice.

Even if he knew that the two of them together would be nothing short of a fiery explosion.

After what seemed like hours of staring into the fire – but was likely only a few minutes as Eric did not exactly have a long degree of attention – he threw back the covers and lay down on the bed.

He tossed an arm over his eyes as he tried not to focus on the fact that he was now a husband, missing his wife on their wedding night.

He pictured Faith as she had looked that day. Her hair was up, curled, pinned away from her face with just the odd ringlet dropping down.

How that hair had looked with pieces fallen out of its pins as she stood outside, so powerful with the bow in her hands, the muscles in her arms rippling with strength as she drew back the drawstring.

He knew that many men had been surprised when he had told them of his infatuation with Lady Faith. They wondered how he could want a woman so strong, so against submitting herself to a man.

But the truth was, he admired her power – both inside and out.

And he wanted that strength with him, on him, beneath him.

The longer he pictured her in his mind, the more he desired her, until he found his hand wandering down to the waistband of his breeches.

It didn't take more than a couple of strokes for him to be groaning, her name spilling from his lips.

He was so caught up in what he was doing that he didn't see the door open, didn't hear the padding of her footsteps, didn't even note the dip of her weight on the bed.

It wasn't until she spoke that he was made aware of her presence and belatedly noticed all the signs she was approaching that he had missed.

"Need some help?" came her voice, full of laughter and yet thick with desire.

His eyes sprang open to find her sitting in front of him, a smile teasing her lips before her tongue darted out and licked them, her eyes glassy with desire as she stared at him and what he was doing to himself.

"Faith," he ground out, his voice hoarse. "What are you doing here?"

"I came," she said, holding her head up high, "for my wedding night."

* * *

Faith was doing her best to exude confidence that she simply didn't feel.

But as she had lain in bed alone, staring up at the ceiling, she hadn't been able to resist the urge to go to Eric and to be with him as she had fantasized about over and over again.

He was the face of every hero in her books. He was the man who haunted her dreams. He was, annoyingly, persistent in being by her side no matter her protestations.

So she might as well take advantage.

Her heart had thudded against her ribcage as she had padded over the thick rug between their rooms until she stood outside of his bedroom door, looking from one side to the other as though she was about to be caught doing something illicit – which was silly, for Eric was now her husband and, unlike the many other times they had shared a bed, this time it was expected.

The door to his room had creaked as she had pushed it open, only to be greeted by darkness within, but for the soft orange glow cast about the room from the embers burning in the fireplace. She had been able to make out his large frame on the bed, and her breath caught as she wondered whether he even wanted her here.

Then her name had emerged from his lips as a groan of supplication, and it was only then that she had realized he was not still, nor sleeping – but that his hand was moving beneath the black trousers he had worn for the day, the sleeves of his long white linen shirt pushed up as he worked himself back and forth.

A warm flush crept its way up her cheeks as she rigidly stood and watched him, the light dancing off of his cheekbones, his dark hair falling over his face.

When he had murmured her name again, she had started, wondering if he had noticed her. As his eyes had remained closed, however, she had realized that he must be picturing her. She hadn't been able to help but wonder just how he was envisioning her.

She had padded over the hardwood floor to the carpet, sinking softly down beside him on the bed, the silk canopy brushing against her cheek as she did. When she leaned over him, his warmth radiated toward her skin, drawing her ever closer.

He was so handsome, so captivating that she nearly doubted herself and ran from the room before he noticed her presence, and to stop herself, she did the only thing she could think of – which was to do as Eric did himself and introduce some levity to the situation.

"Need some help?" she had asked, and that's when his eyes had flown open and caught hers, surprise within them but not alarm. Surprise which quickly turned to a deep appreciation that caused Faith's cheeks to flush even hotter.

When he had asked her what she was doing there, she had

told him the truth – she was there for her wedding night. He could take that as he wished.

He reached out and cupped her cheek, brushing away a few stray strands of hair that had fallen across her face. His thumb stroked along the curve of her jawline as they stared into each other's eyes, light-heartedness beginning to fade as instead, Faith's hunger for him reflected back at her.

Taking a deep breath to steady her nerves, she leaned forward to kiss him, and before she had barely moved he sat up forcefully, meeting her more than halfway as his hands wrapped around her upper arms to hold her still while his lips took hers prisoner. All he had needed was the invitation. There was never any gentle press of their lips upon each other's – but then, with them, it had never been like that. It had been a fiery passion, whether they had been arguing, kissing, or pursuing the next answer in this treasure hunt of theirs.

His tongue sought hers as he branded her, their surrendering to their need for one another binding them together as much as their vows to one another had.

In one swift motion, Eric lifted Faith up as though she weighed nothing and laid her back on the bed, holding himself above her as his eyes ran over her from top to bottom like he was preparing to eat his favorite dessert before he settled atop her body. His hands were seemingly everywhere as he ran them along her curves, and she ached to be closer to him, to feel his skin upon hers. In this moment, she finally understood the expression of two flesh becoming one, as she was struck by her longing for the warmth of his skin, to touch him as he had been doing to himself.

He either read her thoughts or felt the same, for, with a small groan as he lifted himself from her, he removed his shirt and tossed it aside, giving Faith the chance to take in his defined chest and arms. She had known how large he was of course, but his clothing had hidden what was waiting beneath. She lifted her hands and stroked them over the breadth of his muscles, which were as sculpted as those eternalized in marble from Roman days within the museum. Her fingertips tingled as she skimmed them along the valleys of his chest before lowering them to explore the ridges beneath them.

His hands tangled in her hair as their tongues feverishly explored each other's mouths. He seemed to know just how to move against her in ways that sent shivers down her spine as she gasped in both pleasure and need. The tie of her wrapper had somehow already come undone, and he now impatiently pushed it to the side. Faith couldn't help her grin when he paused as it came off.

She was no young innocent. She had known what to expect when she came in here and had decided that a nightgown was only going to be an inconvenience.

"You were quite sure that I would agree to this, then, were you?" he growled against her lips, and she pushed him up so that she could see his face.

"Are you asking me to leave?" she challenged him, knowing exactly what his answer was going to be.

"Don't you dare," he said, before descending again.

Her hands ran over his back, the sensation of his skin against hers now causing her to arch and cling tightly to him, for, truth be told, she was afraid of being swept away by just how strong her emotions toward him could grow – and how he just might ruin any chance she had to accept a life of independence if it ever came to that in the future.

When he shifted slightly, his hard length pressed against her stomach and their breath mingled together, his musky scent filling her and causing her heart to beat ever faster in anticipation.

Their kisses became hungrier as they deepened, teasing each other's lips, while their bodies moved in perfect harmony. Faith wanted so much more of him that she had to concentrate on containing her excitement within. His hands roamed over every inch of her body, except for the one place she needed them.

Finally, she couldn't take it any longer and she hooked her leg around him, drawing him down so that his hips were firmly pressed against her.

"Wait," he said, panting, his forehead damp. "You're not ready."

"I think I know when I am ready," she returned forcefully. "And ready I am."

Eric shook his head before his hands finally reached the place she had been waiting for him. He expertly slid two fingers inside of her as his thumb massaged her above, and Faith gasped as her head rolled back in pleasure.

"Fine," he said as he only intensified his caresses. "Maybe you were right."

"I am always right," she ground out. "But don't stop."

He didn't listen but instead, after one more deep kiss, rolled them over so that now she was on top.

"What are you doing?" she asked, hating that he knew so much that she didn't, but when he lifted his hands to cup her face, he made her feel as though she was the only woman he had ever done this with.

"I'm giving you control," he said as he positioned her above him. "Take what you need."

With her hands on his chest, Faith pushed herself up so that she was poised above him and, with his hands on her hips, guiding her but not pushing her, she lowered herself down upon him. She did so slowly, taking in an inch of him every few seconds before he was seated within her and she stopped, gasping at how full she felt.

"You are so wet. So tight," Eric mumbled as he stared up at her. "Move when you're ready."

She took some experimental thrusts, each one feeling more comfortable until comfort turned into pleasure that began to move through her, stars dancing behind her eyes.

Eric began to move with her, each propulsion pulling them higher together.

He reached up, caressing her breasts and teasing her nipples, creating sensations unlike anything Faith had ever felt before, and soon she found her movements becoming more frenzied.

Eric's hands left her hips and wrapped around her back as each thrust brought them closer and closer to the edge they both needed to reach.

Their breath quickened, their skin glistening in sweat as Eric moved one of his hands down between them, pushing against her until his thumb found just the right spot, sending her over the edge, giving her what she had been longing for but had been unable to find. With one final forward motion, she went tumbling into blissful oblivion as everything faded away into nothing but pleasure.

Eric tensed beneath her until he pulsed inside of her while he squeezed her hips as though he would never let go.

And she hoped, with everything she had, that he never would.

CHAPTER 21

"That was amazing," Eric said huskily, stroking Faith's hair as she lay with her head on his chest, their bodies still entwined as her leg was thrown over his.

The pleasure had faded, but his desire for her had not. He knew, however, that this was her first time and he didn't want her to feel forced into doing anything more than she wanted to.

Faith looked up at him, her blue eyes soft and dreamy, a lazy smile playing on her lips. Eric had to tell his heart to be still when he saw the emotion in her eyes as she stared up at him – an adoration that, until this point, she had kept hidden.

He nodded, his fingers lazily tracing circles on her hip as he pulled her closer to him.

"It was," he said, pressing a kiss to the top of her head before continuing. "Because it was with you."

She dipped her head as she nodded against him, and even though she didn't go anywhere, he could feel her slipping away.

"What is it?" he asked.

"Nothing."

"Faith," he said as sternly as he could. "I am your husband now, so if I ask, you must tell me. You are to obey me, remember?"

When she looked up and caught his eyes, he couldn't keep it in anymore, and he started to laugh. She joined in with a chuckle, although she sobered more quickly than he.

"The truth is… it *was* amazing. I suppose I just can't help but think that it was so amazing because you have such a great deal of experience in all of this."

An ache began in Eric's chest that, after what they had shared, her thoughts would go to his past.

He pushed himself up to a sitting position, lifting her so that he could clearly see her face.

"Faith," he said, all levity gone. "I need you to understand something."

She said nothing, looking at him with some suspicion from beneath her lashes as he continued.

"Yes, I have been with other women," he said as her eyes narrowed. "But none of them mattered. That was just a physical coming together. You and I… well, it's more than that. It has meaning to it. This was us binding ourselves to one another. A promise. A commitment. A—"

He was about to tell her a show of love, but the thought shocked him enough that he wasn't sure what it would do to her.

She lifted a brow, waiting.

"A beginning," he finished instead. "A beginning of a new life together. One which is just you and me, against whatever comes our way. Before you came into the room, you know that I was thinking of you, do you not?"

She nodded nearly imperceptibly.

"You are all I think of. You are all I want. I cannot change my past, but my future is yours."

He reached out and took her hands in his, which, to him, was nearly as intimate as what they had shared before. "Now, I have tired you out. Time to sleep."

He saw her hesitation and wondered at it, until she asked, "Should I sleep here or in my room?"

He grinned as he swept an arm around and pulled her to him. "Here, of course. What kind of question is that?"

"Very well," she said, her smile evident just before she hid it.

"Now, I have one more problem."

"Which is?"

"I never did find that tickle spot."

She gasped and began to scootch back away from him, but he grinned and chased her on hands and knees across the bed.

He caught her, clasping her wrists in one hand when she lifted them to defend herself. He ran the fingers of his other hand up and down her sides, searching for that one spot that would make her squirm.

She wriggled in his arms, giggling uncontrollably as his fingers danced across her skin. Her laughter was like music and he smiled at her unrestricted show of joy.

When he used both hands to tickle her sensitive sides, she suddenly grabbed them and pulled him towards her. Their lips met in a fiery kiss, filled with the passion and desire they had been holding back for so long and finally released tonight.

When her nails dug into his shoulders, he no longer held on so tightly but instead laid her back on the bed, his need for her unabated from their first round.

He lifted himself from her mouth, his breath hot and fast as he looked into her eyes.

"Are you ready again?" he asked, and she nodded, her

hands coming to his cheeks and pulling him back in toward her.

"Are you sure?" he persisted, aware of how soon it was after her first time, even as the perspiration from holding himself back began to drip down his brow.

"Eric," she said, her voice harsh. "I would tell you no if that is what I felt."

He nodded once. That was all he needed to hear, for he knew it was the truth. Faith would never agree to anything she had no interest in.

This time when he took her, he didn't go slow or make love to her. He sunk into her with a groan, pausing when he heard her gasp. He was about to pull out when she shook her head, her nails digging into his ass as she held him against her.

"Don't stop," she said, and he pulled out just enough to thrust in again, her cry of pleasure encouraging him. He continued, faster and faster until her head was thrown back, her mouth gaping open and her eyes glossy.

"That's it," she whimpered, and when she tightened around him gloriously, he spent into her with a roar.

He hadn't lied to her. It had never been like this with anyone else, and there was no reason he would ever need anyone else again.

She was his. Just as he was hers.

Now he just had to make sure she believed it.

* * *

"I will miss you terribly, you do know that?"

Faith was sitting with Hope the next morning. She had left Eric lying languidly in his bed, his eyes still half-closed. He had watched her dress in her nightclothes and return to her room with hooded eyes that told her he likely would have been happy to make love again, but she was a bit too sore from their rounds last night – although she wasn't complaining.

She had told him she was hungry and he had offered to call for breakfast, but somehow asking for servants in the home she had grown up in to serve her in her husband's bedroom seemed scandalous, even though she knew it was not only perfectly acceptable but expected.

She supposed it was going to take some time to shift from her role of an innocent young lady to a married woman who could do as she pleased.

She hoped that Eric would understand her need to look after herself and not completely adhere to that "obey" part of the vows.

"I am going to miss you too," Faith said now, reaching out and covering her sister's hand in her own.

Hope's brows lifted slightly, likely in surprise at Faith showing any affection, but such absence from her sister had been difficult.

"We are not so far away, you know," Hope said. "You are welcome to my home any time you would like."

"We were apart for some time already," Faith said. "It's not so different from you marrying."

"I suppose not," Hope said with a smile that didn't quite reach her eyes. For a moment, Faith wondered if Hope was worried about the distance between them, but she realized there was more than that.

"Hope, what is it?" she asked.

"Nothing," Hope said quickly – too quickly. Faith knew better than to fall for the act that everyone else would.

"Hope…"

"I had only envisioned that you might come live with me, is all," Hope said with a shrug of her shoulders. "If you had never married, that is, for you were always so adamantly against it. But I am happy that you have found someone."

She patted Faith's hand before removing hers.

Faith narrowed her eyes. "You do not think I am going to be happy, do you?"

"Oh, Faith, I never said that," Hope said, her eyes widening.

"Tell me the truth, Hope, please," Faith said, her stomach swirling in unease. Hope was the ever-optimist, the eternal believer in love. If she was questioning Faith's marriage, what did that mean about her husband? "Do you not think that Eric will be satisfied with me?"

"Faith," Hope said earnestly, leaning forward. "What you need to remember is that you are the most amazing woman there ever was. I do hope – I *believe* – that he sees it. He was so eager to marry you and has been infatuated with you ever since you told him no. You are just so dear to me that I will always fear you being hurt."

"*You* are worried about *me*?" Faith said, taken aback. She had always been the older sister, the one watching out for Hope. She had never considered that Hope might have any concern for her.

Hope looked from one side to the other to make sure no one else had arrived and then leaned in, lowering her voice so the servants in the room wouldn't hear.

"I have seen the way you look at your husband. You love him."

Faith said nothing, even as her heart started pumping hard. Love. She hadn't considered it. She enjoyed Eric's company and was certainly attracted to him but love… could it be true?

"Lord Ferrington is popular with the ladies and I know how you were hurt in the past. I would never want to see you turned away from love like that again," Hope said, biting her lip. "I would like to believe that he will be true to you, but perhaps give it some time before you fully trust him. He was chasing you for so long that I suppose I just want to be certain that it is more than the chase that has fueled him."

Faith sat there in stunned silence, but she had no opportunity to respond as Percy and her husband – Eric's brother, Noah Rowley – joined them. It was certainly not a conversation to be had in front of them. She pasted a wooden smile on her face to greet them.

Had she been wrong all along, blindly believing what she wanted to hear? And had she already lost her heart?

* * *

Eric stretched his arms wide across the silk sheets as he sunk into the feather mattress, enjoying the relaxation in his muscles after being so well and deliciously used last night. The smile stretched just as wide as he remembered all that he and Faith had shared.

Faith. His wife.

He threw his legs over the side of the bed, shaking his head incredulously. Two years ago, there had been a moment when he had caught a glimpse of what he could have – with Faith. After her rejection of him, he had never considered this with another, and now… here she was.

Well, not here at the moment. He recalled through his sleepy haze that she had said something about going down to breakfast.

He called for his valet, who helped him dress. Even the servant commented on the spring in his step.

"It is a good day," Eric said, smiling at himself in the mirror. "A very good day, indeed."

He wondered how long they were going to stay here at Newfield. He knew Faith was happy here and was enjoying visiting with her family – especially her sister – but he was looking forward to returning home and starting their life together, after a quick stop to return the compass and the map to Castleton.

He remembered his mother and his smile faltered slightly. She was as strong of a presence as Faith was herself. He could only hope that the two women he loved most in the world would learn to get along well together.

Love. There was that word again.

He was falling for Faith. But would she ever feel the same?

CHAPTER 22

"We shall be at Castleton before sunset," Eric said, staring at his wife from across the carriage. They had finally left Newfield, and not a moment too soon, for he was getting itchy from having to share her time.

His mother was returning to Newfield and would ensure it was prepared for their arrival.

Home, where they would begin their lives together. He could not wait to show Faith his family's country home, to make it theirs.

But first, he had to determine why she was being so distant.

"It has been convenient to live so close to Castleton," she said, distracting him. "I wish Cassandra had been in residence more often when we were young. Isn't it interesting that we first came to know her in London, and yet were so close all this time?"

"Well, it is fortunate that everything came about the way it did, for it all led to us being together," he said, lifting her hand and bringing it to his lips, kissing the back of it.

"Yes," was all she said, her small smile not quite reaching her eyes, concerning him.

"We shall stop for something to eat at the inn mid-day."

"I am sure we can make it all the way," she said, her brow furrowing, but he shook his head.

"I should like some time alone with you," he said. "From the moment we were actually married, we have been surrounded by other people."

"Our families."

"Yes," he said. "I do have to ask… are you happy? Ever since our wedding night, you have been rather subdued."

Eric knew that his words might be dangerous, but he had to say them anyway. It had been a week since their wedding, and their stay at Newfield had been… routine. He couldn't complain – how could he when Faith had been in his bed each night or he had been in hers – but at this point, he would almost trade the camaraderie they had shared when travelling to Spain and back together, without any of the physical intimacy, to what they had now.

The Eric of a few months ago would have laughed at such a thought.

While they spent their nights together, their days were primarily apart. He understood. Faith wanted to be with her family every moment possible before she left them, which provided him the opportunity to pass the time with his brother and Whitehall, but still… he had missed her.

He studied her from across the carriage. Her head was tilted upon her long neck as she stared out the window at the scenery passing by. Damn, but she was beautiful. Her features were strong, yet fit together perfectly.

As perfect as she was for him.

She turned her head to look at him now, and he almost lost himself in the ocean of her eyes.

"I will miss my family," she said, busying her hands in her skirts. "Especially my sister."

He leaned forward and took her hand in his. "You can see her whenever you wish," he said. "Just say the word."

"Thank you," she returned with a small smile.

Eric cleared his throat, unsure how to say the next words without further upsetting her. She was already missing her family, so perhaps it was not the best time, but he had never been one to hold back on what he was thinking.

"I feel as though you are keeping yourself at a distance from me."

"Why do you think that?" she asked, but the telltale dance of her fingertips upon her knee gave her away.

"Can't say exactly," he said. "But it seems as though things have been rather stilted. Even when you hated me, it was with such a fiery passion. Now you seem to have turned off that part of you."

"You want me to hate you again?"

"I want you to show me who you truly are and not hold yourself back."

She dipped her head now and when she finally looked up at him, the sheen of wetness covering her eyes took him aback.

"But what if you do not like what you see?" she said, her voice near a whisper as she was no longer able to disguise her fear. "What if, now that you have me, you tire of me? Or worse, grow to resent me?"

"Why would I ever resent you?"

"Because you are stuck with me and me alone."

Eric couldn't take this melancholy self-pity of hers anymore. He leaned over, his arms coming beneath her and lifting her onto his side of the carriage.

"I would like nothing better than to be stuck to you," he said with a grin.

"Eric!" she gasped as she settled on his lap. "We are in a moving carriage."

"All the better," he said, laying her down beneath him, as cumbersome as it was on the squab that was too short for her height.

"You do know that not all problems can be solved this way," she said sternly, but Eric was pleased to see that he had achieved his aim of causing her tears to disappear.

He trailed a finger along her cheek. "If only they could," he said mischievously but then sobered when he saw the seriousness in her eyes. "I know they cannot," he said. "But it didn't seem my words were working to convince you that you are all that I want, so I thought that I would show you instead."

She quirked an eyebrow. "You have been quite the demonstrator until now."

"There is always more to explore," he said. "Even the most travelled road can make for the greatest of journeys."

She stared at him for a moment before her lips parted. "Are you calling me well-used?"

He threw back his head and laughed. "Not yet, love. But you will be – by me. Only me."

The endearment fell out of his mouth before he even realized what he was saying, but she didn't comment upon it. Before she could respond, he leaned down and kissed her, sealing his lips over hers.

This woman drove him crazy. But he was telling the truth when he said that he wouldn't have it any other way.

The carriage jostled them as Eric deepened the kiss, his tongue exploring the inside of her mouth while his hands roamed her body. She moaned into him, her fingers tangling in his hair as she pulled him closer. The sound of the wheels on the cobblestones outside was a distant hum as they lost themselves in each other.

Eric broke the kiss, trailing his lips along her jawline to her neck. He drew back the fabric of her gown to nip at her skin, leaving marks that would last for days but would be visible only to him. She arched her back, offering herself to him, and he knew that despite the shields she had raised, deep inside she wanted him as much as he did her.

He obliged, sliding his hand under her dress, feeling the wetness between her legs, which only fueled his desire. He couldn't get enough of her.

He leaned back, pulling her up with him so that she was straddling him, her dress bunched up around her hips. She looked down at him, her eyes dark with desire, and he knew that she understood exactly what he was about to do.

He dipped two fingers inside of her, causing her to gasp. She threw her head back, her hands clutching the fabric of his breeches for support. He loved watching her, loved knowing that he was the one who had put that look in her eyes, that he could make her feel like this. She might not be able to say how she felt in words yet, but her body spoke volumes.

He continued stroking her insides, increasing the speed of his fingers as she started to tighten around them.

When her breath turned to gasps, he knew she was close. He wanted to feel her tighten around him, needed to hear her scream his name.

She let out a keening cry, and he could feel her release around his fingers.

He slowed, wanting badly to unfasten his fall and lift her over top of him, but he stopped himself. He had wanted to show her how he felt, not ask for anything of her in this moment.

Faith reached down to release him, but he stopped her, holding onto her fingers as he looked into her eyes.

"That was for you," he said. "My gift."

"But—"

"No buts," he said gently.

Faith slid off his lap and their eyes met and held as the carriage slowly bumped along. It wasn't until the door opened behind them, causing them both to gasp, that Eric realized they had come to a stop.

"My lord?" The footman said, clearing his throat. "We have arrived at the inn if you would still like to stop."

"Yes, of course," Eric said, stepping out of the carriage before reaching up and offering Faith his hand. He hadn't undressed her, but still, she appeared slightly dishevelled and when he noted the redness of her cheeks, he smiled, proud of himself for putting it there.

He held his arm out, privileged to lead such a beautiful woman inside – as his wife in truth this time.

The tavern in front of them was a modest, timber-framed building, with a thatched roof and a signboard outside welcoming all to The Sword and Thistle, in words as well as a rather impressive pictorial. Beside the door were garden beds that were beginning to turn yellow with the season, and the windows were covered in curtains that held a great deal of soot.

"Have you been here before?" Faith asked, and Eric nodded.

"A few times. It is a common stopping place when travelling to Castleton. I am assuming you have?"

"Of course."

"Lady Faith." A portly gentleman walked over to them, holding his hands out. "It has been some time since I have seen you."

"Mr. Johns," Faith greeted him. "It is good to see you. Lord Ferrington, this is Mr. Johns, the innkeeper. My husband, Lord Ferrington."

The man turned wide eyes onto Eric as he broke out into a smile.

"I had not realized our Lady Faith – my apologies, Lady Ferrington – had married."

"We are travelling to Castleton and were hoping for a meal," Faith said, and the man instantly began to move.

"Of course, of course. Right this way. The best table for you. For both of you."

Eric couldn't help but smile at the man's obvious complete adoration of Faith, nearly tripping over himself as he led them into the lively, warm room, dimly lit despite the hour of the day. Filled with wood smoke and travellers, the room's fireplace shed its light and heat upon the many people gathered within.

"Here we are," the innkeeper said as they came to one of the scarred, sturdy wooden tables and benches that was, so far, empty. "Mutton's on today."

They nodded their thanks before he departed, and each of them surveyed the room, Eric scanning to ensure that all appeared safe.

His gaze was stopped by a woman walking toward them. There was something about her that tugged at his memory, but Eric had no clear indication of her identity.

He shrugged, dismissing her, before turning back to Faith. He had been honest in wanting to continue their conversation – the one they had been avoiding. He hated to have anything unresolved hanging over him.

When he set his attention upon her, however, all of the words escaped him at the look on her face, as though she had seen a ghost.

Eric followed her gaze to see that the woman had stopped beside them – and not only stopped but was now sliding onto the bench. On his side.

"Lady Montgomery," Faith said icily. "How surprising to see you."

"And you Lady Faith. I didn't know you had married."

"She is Lady Ferrington now," Eric interjected, annoyed at the interruption. "And you are?"

Lady Montgomery looked from Faith to Eric and back again as a much older, portly gentleman trundled in behind her – a man Eric recognized.

Lord Montgomery. Was he this woman's father? He didn't know him well, but he attended Parliament and social events. The man had been his father's age. However, Faith had called this woman Lady Montgomery…

Eric nodded his greetings, even as confusion filled him.

"You are travelling with your husband, I see," Faith said, nodding to the man who Eric had assumed was her father.

"I am."

"I am sorry," Eric said, interjecting, scratching his temple. "But who are you?"

It wasn't the woman who answered, however. It was Faith herself.

"Eric, this is Lady Montgomery, and I am surprised you could forget her."

"Oh?" he said, raising a brow and turning to Faith. "Why is that?"

"Because she is the woman you carried on with that night. The night you left me."

CHAPTER 23

Faith was in shock. How could he not remember Lady Montgomery? The last she had seen of the woman, she and Eric had been locked in an embrace in an alcove.

She was as beautiful as ever, her large, expressive blue-green eyes twinkling above her well-defined cheekbones, which were accentuated when she smiled, as she was right now. She was a captivating woman – she had been ever since they were young – and Faith didn't blame Eric for being attracted to her, even if she was married.

"Lord Montgomery," Eric said when the man approached, although Lord Montgomery made no move to join them on the bench. Faith recalled that Lady Montgomery's match had been one made for power and certainly not of her choosing. "How are you?"

"Fine," Lord Montgomery said dismissively. "I'll be at the bar."

He walked, away, leaving his wife behind.

"Is this a joke?" Eric asked both women.

Faith stared back at him incredulously, noting that Lady

Montgomery did the same, although her expression was accompanied by much more amusement than Faith's.

"I am sorry, Lady Montgomery, but I do not recall any time together with you."

"You'd had a fair bit of whiskey that night, it's true," she said, her voice warm and melodic. Faith had never had an issue with her until that evening, and she hated how petty she was for disliking the woman now. "Do not worry, Lady Ferrington. I have no interest in taking your husband away from you. I am usually more interested in having fun since I am married myself and all. Did the two of you marry for love or…"

She let the remainder of the thought dangle in the air, and Faith understood. She was asking if she had permission to have some "fun" with Eric again.

She knew he would deny her. How could he not, when Faith was sitting right next to him? But she also knew that he likely wanted to tell Lady Montgomery otherwise. Lady Montgomery was beautiful, experienced, vivacious, flirtatious – everything that Faith wasn't.

If they had married for love, then perhaps she could believe that Eric wanted her and only her.

But she had trapped him into this marriage, whether she had meant to or not.

He hadn't asked her to join him on the ship, but once she had, he'd had no choice but to stay with her to keep her safe.

She had sealed their fates and now he was stuck with her.

Faith couldn't take it a moment longer.

"If you might excuse me," she said before sliding to the edge of the bench, her skirts catching on the edge as she did so rapidly. Eric was watching her with worried eyes and stood along with her, but before he could say anything she turned and fled, the innkeeper calling her name as she pushed open the heavy timber door and hurried down the cobblestones.

Lady Montgomery likely thought her gone mad, but Faith didn't care any longer. She had no idea where she was going. She just had to go somewhere – anywhere – away.

"Faith!"

Eric's low voice vibrated toward her, and she lifted her skirts and hurried away as fast as she could, even though the rational part of her mind told her that there was no way she could ever outrun him. His legs were too long, his stride was too strong, and his resolve would be too determined.

She was trapped, just as much as he was. Why wouldn't he just let her go?

Faith finally stopped when she reached a clearing on the edge of the small town, unable to continue any longer. Her lungs were heavy and her breathing fast. She threw one arm across her forehead as Eric's footsteps thundered behind her. When he caught her, he didn't touch her, but just stood behind her, waiting.

His breathing was hardly even heavy. Of course.

"Faith?" he finally said, his voice tentative. "Where are you going?"

"Away."

"From me?" he said, his voice almost breaking, and Faith's resolve wobbled for a moment.

"From the reminder of who you are. Of what you could have if I wasn't holding you back."

"Faith, I do not even remember that woman or know who she is. I only recognize her husband, who was a friend of my father's."

"I know," Faith said, finally turning around and allowing her hands to fall at her side. "That is entirely the problem."

"Faith," Eric said, scratching his forehead. "I am so confused."

She sighed. "I know you are." She reached out and picked up his hand, leading him over to a large rock, taking a seat beside him while the sun's rays reached them both, warming them. She wished they could stay here forever.

"Explain to me what I have done wrong."

"Nothing," Faith said, blinking away the tears that burned the back of her eyes that he thought this was somehow his fault. "You have done absolutely nothing wrong. It is me. I am the problem."

"You are not a problem, Faith."

She turned to him, then, meeting his hazel eyes, the color of tea with a generous serving of cream. He was so handsome it was hard to believe that he was hers. But was he, in truth?

"I saw that woman kissing you that night but a short time after I did myself. When I kissed you, it meant everything to me. You were the first and last man I ever kissed. But you have been with so many women that your kiss with her does not even register. We suit one another, yes, but it is hard to believe that I will always be enough for you. You have a past, one that is full of women who warmed your bed and satisfied you. I simply read books about it. You are warm, caring, the light of every room, and I am the opposite in every way. How can I possibly ever be enough for you? And do you want me to be when you could have women such as Lady Montgomery?"

He blinked but didn't say anything right away. "Do you truly think that about yourself?" he finally asked slowly.

She straightened her spine. "I know that I have a lot to offer. I do. I do not pity myself nor believe anything poorly about who I am. I have learned that I am better than that. But I still do not know how any one woman can make up for all of the women you had before."

"Yes, there were women," he said, coming to kneel in

front of her. "But there was only one woman who ever stood out. When I was with the rest of them it was only because I was trying to fill the hole you had left."

Faith's heart began to beat faster, warming as her stomach churned and her mind swam with possibilities. Was it time that she forgot the past and looked forward to the future? Should she continue to guard her heart? Or was it already too late?

"Eric—"

"Lord Ferrington! Lady Ferrington!"

They both turned, surprised to find the carriage awaiting them as close as the road would allow. The driver was standing, calling out to them.

"The painting!" was all they heard, and they exchanged a look before racing to the carriage.

"What about the painting?" Eric asked. They hadn't told the driver it was a map, of course, and had debated leaving it behind, but nor did they want to bring it with them into a crowded tavern. They had decided to ask Eric's valet and driver to guard it for them.

"It is gone."

"Gone?" Eric said in disbelief. "How?"

"I left for but a moment," his valet said from where he sat atop with the driver, panic on his face. "When I returned, it was missing. Someone must have come from behind the driver to capture it."

Eric's hands came to his head as he began to pace back and forth. "What do we do?" he said, looking to Faith. "Ashford will be devastated. We cannot return to Castleton empty-handed."

"Castleton," Faith murmured before her eyes flew up to meet Eric's. "That's it – Castleton. We have to continue."

"But how can we without—"

"If someone wanted to use the map, where would they

THE LORD'S COMPASS

go?" she asked. "They have to be headed toward Castleton. And if they were daring enough to risk stealing the map in the middle of the day from our carriage, what else might they be bold enough to do?"

"Let's go," he said, immediately agreeing.

He helped Faith into the carriage before giving the driver instructions to make for Castleton as fast as they were able.

"Your meals are wrapped inside for you," the valet said, but neither Faith nor Eric was hungry.

Faith wasn't sure if she was glad that their conversation had been interrupted or if it would have been better had they finished it.

She had realized the truth as she had spoken to Eric. The past was part of it, but before now, she had always had the option to leave. She could have been hurt, yes, but she hadn't been tied to whatever had brought her down.

Now? She was vulnerable because of their marriage. It meant that Eric could do as he pleased, and this time, there was nowhere for her to run.

He no longer had the thrill of the chase, but he did have all of the power.

This, however, was not the time to decide what to do next. Now, they had to decide just how they were going to get the map back.

"The compass," Faith said, suddenly remembering it. "Did they get the compass too?"

Eric smiled wryly as he shook his head, reaching into his jacket before pulling the compass out from a pocket.

"Right here," he said. "I figured that not only should I keep it safe, but it might help for me to have something to point me in the right direction."

Faith couldn't help but snicker at that. Nothing could help guide this man. Not when it came to directions.

While Faith knew they didn't have far to go, the rest of

the carriage ride was interminable, both of them sitting on the edge of their seats, watching out the window.

Suddenly the carriage slowed, and Faith craned her neck to see if they were close to Castleton, but no estate loomed in the distance, nor were there any signs of the massive gardens that surrounded it.

"My lord, there is a carriage stopped ahead," came the driver's voice, and Eric was out of the carriage before it even finished rolling to a stop.

"Do you see anyone?" he asked, his voice slightly muffled from outside, and Faith followed him out, picking her steps more carefully so she didn't trip over her skirts.

"No sign of anyone," the driver said. "Should we continue?"

Eric looked back and exchanged a glance with Faith.

"It could be them," she said in a low voice, and he nodded.

"Do we have pistols?" Eric asked, and the driver's eyes widened but he reached into the box and pulled them out before passing them to Eric, who placed them into the waistband of his breeches. "Faith, stay in the carriage."

"But—"

He turned to her, more fire and determination in his eyes than she had ever seen before. "Stay in the carriage."

"Very well," she said, realizing she wasn't going to win this argument. She could do as he said, however, and still do as she wished. He wouldn't like it, but she was not about to sit in the carriage waiting helplessly.

She returned to the carriage, watching out the window until he was no longer in her view before opening the door and emerging once more. She would stay with the carriage, yes, but she would also be prepared.

"Please take our bags down," she said to the driver, who stared uncertainly at her.

"My lady, I am not sure—"

"I am not asking you to take our belongings down from the carriage. I am telling you," she said in clipped tones to remind the driver just who was in charge here.

"Very well," he said reluctantly.

"Can you see my husband?" Faith asked the valet, who shook his head.

"He is on the other side of the carriage."

"How close are we to Castleton?"

"Not far at all. Just a few miles."

Faith nodded as she went to her things and searched until she found what she was looking for. Then she returned to her carriage to wait and see if she just might be needed.

CHAPTER 24

*E*ric slowed his steps as he approached the abandoned carriage. By its size and lack of adornment, he guessed it was hired, not a private coach. The driver's seat was empty and the coach was sitting ajar, while the horses pranced, lifting their hooves as they waited to be commanded. When Eric rounded the side, it was as he expected – one of the wheels had fallen off and it was resting upon its axel.

"Is anyone there?" he called out as he approached, one hand on a pistol behind his back. There was one advantage to his father being a soldier – he had taught both Eric and Noah how to shoot, even if Noah had not been particularly adept or interested.

But Eric had taken to it, a skill for which he was now grateful.

He looked back at his carriage – where Faith awaited him – and while he couldn't see the occupants, it helped to know she was close.

Holding the pistol in front of him, he reached out and flung open the door of the carriage, prepared to face whoever was within – but it was empty. He leaned inside, searching throughout for anything of note, but there was nothing.

Holstering his pistol, he pushed back from the abandoned carriage, about to leave it behind, when he heard a shout in the distance.

He jumped out, his head snapping back as he turned around to see where the source of the concern came from. His heart started to pound rapidly when he realized that it was from behind him – from his own carriage.

From this distance, he could see his driver atop the carriage, two people below it – and from their stance, he guessed they were holding the driver and likely the valet at gunpoint.

He could only hope that they hadn't discovered Faith was within.

Eric took off into a run toward the carriage, hoping he could reach them in time. His lungs burned as it seemed he couldn't move fast enough, and he could only watch helplessly as the driver and valet stepped down from the top of the box.

These men were going to steal his carriage. But what would they do when they discovered Faith?

As Eric approached, he could make out a package under one man's arm, and he wondered if it just might be the map.

He was still too far to do anything when he saw one of them approach the side and open the door.

"Stop!" he called out as loud as he could, hoping to draw their attention away. They both turned to him, but then after a flurry of words in Spanish, one of them pointed his gun at him while the other remained where he was.

Eric lifted his pistol and fired at the exact moment the man shot at him. He flinched as the bullet whizzed by him, swearing when he realized his own had also missed. With no time to reload the pistol, he grabbed the other one, hoping he would have an advantage over the other man. They both were distracted, however, when the second man went flying backward with a cry, landing on his back beside the carriage – with an arrow sticking out of his chest.

"Carlos, are you hurt?" the man yelled in Spanish as he crouched down next to him, and Eric finally drew close enough to determine the identity of his opponent – *Don* Raphael himself.

Don Raphael turned, and Eric lifted his gun toward him, although he was overcome with confusion at the smile widening on the man's face.

"Something amusing?" Eric asked wryly.

"Sí," said *Don* Raphael, and at the prickle in his spine, Eric turned around slowly, only to find another three men standing behind him, pistols raised.

"You do not seem to have any choices remaining," *Don* Raphael said in English with a smirk that caused Eric's ire to grow ever larger. "Put down the gun, and, *señora*, I would suggest you set that bow down before you hurt yourself."

That was not going to go over well with Faith.

Little did *Don* Raphael know that Faith could likely wield the weapon better than the rest of them combined.

"Here is what is going to happen," *Don* Raphael said. "My men and I are going to take this carriage and continue to Castleton with the painting that you stole from me."

Eric didn't respond. As long as they released Faith, nothing else mattered.

"And we are going to take your pretty wife with us," he said with a snarl that had Eric jumping forward toward him until one of the Spaniards caught him and pulled him back.

"You are *not* taking my wife," Eric said desperately.

"You do not have a say in the matter," *Don* Raphael said. "You came to my country, to my house, you pretended to be someone you were not, and you stole from me. You may have found a clue, but you will not be keeping the treasure. I have come for what is rightfully mine."

"Is it, though?" Eric challenged him, hoping that if he kept him talking for long enough, someone would pass by and help them. "From what I am told, it was never yours to begin with."

"Neither is it yours," *Don* Raphael said. "I feel, however, that I am missing something that would allow me to better understand what I am looking at. I can only hope that your pretty bride can provide me with the answers. For if she cannot, then I will have no use for her and you both shall be punished for what you have done to me."

"Now see here—"

"Farewell!" *Don* Raphael called out in a singsong voice.

Eric knew the odds were stacked against him, but he wasn't going to let the Spaniards get away with Faith. He charged forward, hoping he could take *Don* Raphael off guard and knock him off of his feet – but as he did, he heard the shot from behind him, followed by searing pain in his calf along with a woman's cry of distress that must have been Faith even if he had never imagined her in such desperation – and he collapsed, no matter how hard he tried to stay upright.

"Faith," he groaned as the wheels beside him began to move with a creak, and as all hope left him, he prayed with everything within him that Faith would be kept safe. And wished that he had told her just how much he loved her.

* * *

FAITH WAS NOT one to cry. She was not one to panic. She was the type of woman who would look at the situation in front of her, no matter how desperate, and decide on the best course forward.

However, she had never been in a situation quite this dire, where it was very likely it might not end with her alive.

She thought she would have been able to handle it with a relative degree of resolve – until Eric had been shot. Now she was fighting tears and doing what she could to prevent herself from losing all sense of reason as she wondered what had happened to him – how badly he had been hit, and whether he was still even alive. She blinked rapidly at the thought that she might now truly be without him as a hole in her chest began to grow.

She would be of no help to him if she collapsed into a puddle. All she could do was get help for him – and get it quickly.

She gritted her teeth. She was not about to go down without fighting, and she knew her fighting would have to be quick.

She stared at the three men who surrounded her, one who held a pistol aimed at her. They likely were not at all threatened by her, but instead, they were using her as leverage to keep the driver following their orders. Faith had protested, telling the driver not to listen to them, but she could understand his perspective. He was not about to appear at Castleton with the news that his disobedience had gotten her killed.

Then *Don* Raphael had ordered one of the Spaniards to sit up top to ensure that his instructions were followed.

Faith twisted her hand around the solid wood she held within it, running her thumb over the sharp edge at the end of it. She had no idea how she could combat the three of them, but she was ready to do whatever was needed of her.

Suddenly, the carriage lurched forward and Faith stumbled, losing her balance but catching herself on the seat behind her. Her captors were similarly surprised and in the few short extra seconds it took them to find their footing, she took full advantage.

She shot forward as quickly as she could, turning her shoulder so that her entire body crashed into the man in front of her. He went flying backward, hitting the wall of the carriage as she did. She flinched as she followed after him, ending up on the floor at his feet – but she wasn't done.

She quickly snatched her bow and arrows from the floor beside her, throwing her quiver on her back as she turned to face the second man. He had already regained his footing, and the first attacker surprised her by grabbing her from behind, wrapping his arms around her waist as he picked her up and held her, apparently as a gift for *Don* Raphael. The Spaniard smiled evilly as he watched her grapple with his men, and Faith wished with all her might that she had trusted her instinct the first time she had seen him. But it was too late for that now.

The first man had her by the waist, but he hadn't held her hands – which was a huge mistake on his part. For as soon as *Don* Raphael neared, she lifted her hand and pressed the broken piece of arrow forward, wincing as she felt it pierce into his shoulder muscle.

"Ahhh! You bitch!" he yelled out and the man who held Faith yanked her back away from him and began to fight her for the quiver of arrows she now clutched to her.

"That was for Eric!" she cried. "Now, open the carriage and release me!"

"Never," *Don* Raphael snarled as he slapped his right hand to his left shoulder where Faith had stabbed him. "Do you truly believe that you can overcome all of us?"

He was right – there was no way that she could. But she was sure going to try.

Just as she launched herself forward, the carriage door

was thrown open, and two men with their faces covered stood in the doorway with pistols drawn.

Highwaymen? Were they truly going to be robbed now, when it seemed as though all had already been taken from her?

"Out!" One of the men shouted, and Faith stumbled forward, the other men following her.

"Hand over your weapons," the second man said in a voice that, while muffled, tugged at Faith's memories. She'd heard that voice before – although where escaped her. It was none of the men involved in this treasure hunt, however, of that she was certain.

She was about to pass over her bow and arrows when one of the highwaymen held out a hand, palm first, to stop her.

"Run away, Lady Ferrington, as fast as you can," he said, and she started in shock that he knew who she was. Had he arrived to rescue her?

"I-I will, but... my husband, he's... he's..." The pain hit her anew, "injured," she said, panting, not allowing herself to finish the sentence. He could not be anything besides injured. She couldn't go there.

The two men exchanged a look.

"Take the carriage and return for him," one said, nodding to the driver, who sat on top. "We will look after these men."

Faith nodded, her need to return to Eric overcoming her confusion at who these men were and why they were saving her.

Later on, she would consider just why they had done so, but for now, she only had one purpose, and one purpose alone.

To get to Eric and make sure he survived.

CHAPTER 25

⚜

Eric groaned as he opened his eyes, the pain radiating up his leg overwhelming all of his other senses.

He took a breath, pushing away the burning in his lower leg with his resolve to fight through it. He had to find Faith. She was alone with five men – make that four, he realized, when he registered the body lying next to him.

He crawled over toward it using his arms and good leg, and when the body twitched, he jumped backward.

The man was still alive, although blood was pooling on his chest where Faith's arrow had pierced him. Eric looked about, seeing nothing around him but dusty road and trees. And there, in the distance, the shape of Castleton.

He crawled toward the road, hoping that he would be able to attract the attention of a passing carriage, keeping an eye open for a stick or other tool he could use to walk – although perhaps he was being optimistic to think that he could bring himself upright.

Eric couldn't have said how long it took him to make progress, but by the time he reached the road, exhaustion had set in, and when he turned to look behind him he saw with dejection, captured by a trail of blood, that he had barely made any progress.

He wasn't going to make it. That was not what most aggrieved him, however – it was the thought that no one would ever know what happened to Faith, and they would never be able to truly recognize their love for one another. Love that he had been scared of providing her for he was worried she would never find it for him in return.

Maybe they both should have taken a chance on one another – and trusted in themselves to be what the other one needed.

Eric fought as hard as he could to keep going, but his eyes were heavy and his leg immovable. He knew that he was nearing the end of his efforts – and then he heard it.

The clopping of the horse's hooves, the turning of the carriage wheels. Was he only hearing what he was wishing for, or was it reality? And was it friend or foe approaching?

He collapsed to the ground, no longer able to do anything but give in to the darkness that awaited.

* * *

FAITH'S HEART pounded as they approached the last place she had seen Eric. Would he still be there? Would he be... alive?

The driver had sensed the urgency as he encouraged the horses on quickly, and Faith hung her head out the window to see what awaited them.

Her heart seemed to jump out of the window and run down the road by itself when she saw him, recognizing the color of his jacket from where he lay on the side of the road – motionless.

"Eric!" she called out, hitting her hand against the side of the carriage to tell the driver to stop, for she was sure she could run faster than even the horses with the desperation that was currently fueling her.

The carriage couldn't slow fast enough, seconds turning into minutes until she could open the door and run down the stairs, tripping over the bottom one and catching herself just before she fell.

"Eric," she cried out, reaching his side, not recognizing the plaintiveness in her voice.

Something hot and wet dripped onto her hands as she reached out to him, belatedly realizing that they were her own tears.

"Eric!" she repeated, screaming at his still frame, his face so pale and the blood behind him too much. She shook him, willing him to respond to her, to show some kind of reaction that there was still life within him.

When he groaned, relief flooded through her, though she knew that they did not have much time to save him. They had to stop the bleeding.

"Faith?" he murmured, although his eyes remained closed.

"I'm here," she said, leaning down and taking his face in her hands.

"I love you," he whispered before his entire body went limp.

"I love you too," she cried out, willing him to respond again, but it was no use, and she had no idea if she had lost him as her sobs emerged, the emotion too much to hold in any longer.

"Help!" Faith called out, lifting her head to see that the driver and valet were there beside her, ready to do what was required. The valet wrapped a handkerchief around Eric's leg before the two of them lifted him and ran him toward the carriage, Faith following them as closely as she could without impeding their progress.

"We're almost there, my lady," the driver said. They

entered the carriage, Faith taking a seat and lifting Eric's head to hold it steady on her lap, as the men draped the rest of his body over one of the seats. "We will go as fast as possible, so hold on. It will be a bumpy ride."

She nodded her thanks as the valet climbed in next to her, helping her to steady Eric on the seat.

"Our fathers were soldiers together," the valet said, nodding toward Eric. "His father was my father's officer, and he gave him a job when he could no longer fight. I know a bit about treating wounds. We've tied it and with pressure, hopefully, the bleeding will stop, or slow, at least."

"And then?" Faith asked, her heart dropping at the hesitation in the man's eyes.

"I would hope that we can prevent any more blood from being lost," he said. "From my first look, the bullet didn't go too deeply into the muscle, but there is a chance he will lose the leg."

Faith bit her lip, knowing how much that would pain Eric.

"As long as he lives," she said, and the valet nodded, although his expression was grim.

"God willing," he said.

They rolled up to Castleton sooner than Faith had expected, and when the driver opened the doors to the carriage, not only were footmen waiting to help, but Lord Ashford was hurrying down the wide stone steps toward them, concern etched onto his handsome face as he approached.

"Lady Ferrington," he said. "How is he?"

"I do not believe he is very well," she said, her voice breaking.

"I have already sent for the physician," he said as footmen lifted Eric and carried him into the house. He was such a large, strong man that it was difficult to see him like this, so limp and broken.

"He will fight through this, Faith."

She looked up, almost surprised to see Cassandra there. Her friend had entered the carriage without her even noticing, so distracted was she.

She nodded woodenly, not wanting to consider any alternative.

Faith turned to her friend, surprised at the hot wetness flowing down her own face.

"I was so guarded, Cassandra. I was so worried that I would end up hurt, and now…" She choked on the word, and Cassandra shook her head and drew Faith toward her.

"He will get through this. I am sure of it," she said, and Faith shook her head into Cassandra's shoulder, unable to say anything else as she let her emotions release.

Finally, she pushed away, her fingers gripping Cassandra's upper arms.

"Oh, Cassandra, there is so much to tell you. I must go to Eric, but there is danger. Spaniards shot Eric and then these other men came and saved us but I don't know where they are now, and you have your baby here when who knows—oh, goodness, I sound like my mother rambling on."

Cassandra took her arm and patted her hand.

"Come, we'll get it all sorted."

Cassandra led her into Castleton, which truly felt like a warm embrace. It had seen better days, that was for certain, but it was comfortable, and loving care had been given to it. Faith noted the concerned faces she passed, including Cassandra's mother and Lord Covington, Cassandra's husband, but greeting them would have to wait.

She soon found herself in the bedroom where Eric had been placed, and true to his word, Lord Ashford had called the physician. When he arrived, he allowed Faith to stay in the room, but he provided his opinions to Lord Ashford.

"The bullet went through the side of his leg. Took out a chunk of the muscle but didn't hit the bone from what I can tell. The main thing is that the bleeding stops soon and the wound doesn't fester."

"Thank you, doctor," Lord Ashford said, but Faith was not accepting his answer. She jumped out of her chair and stood in front of the door to block the physician's exit.

"Can you not stop the bleeding, then? And what do we do if it *does* fester?" she asked.

"That all must happen on its own," he said without much concern. "If you will excuse me."

Realizing she could not force the man to do anything further, she stepped to the side. As he passed, she watched him leave with despair. Lord Ashford walked over and awkwardly patted her shoulder.

"Ferrington's a strong one," he said. "He'll come through this."

Faith nodded woodenly. "Lord Ashford?" she said, remembering the entire reason they were here. Her words were dull, her interest numb, "I shall tell you the full story later, but you have to know… we found a map, but it was stolen, by the same men who came after us and shot Eric. Then we were stopped by highwaymen, who allowed me to go free, while they remained with our attackers. I know it all sounds so fanciful, but the thing is, the map is gone. I am so sorry. I—"

"It is fine."

"But—"

"Lady Ferrington," he said, stopping her with a hand and staring at her. "You have gone through a great ordeal today, but I do not want you to worry. As it happens, I have the map."

THE LORD'S COMPASS

"You—did you say you had the map?"

He nodded. "Shortly before you arrived, one of my servants found a rolled painting in front of the main doorway. Imagine our surprise when we opened it up and I couldn't help but notice its resemblance to the terrain around Castleton."

"But how…"

"Then my butler told me that he had seen a man from a distance, who called out and told him to prepare for an injured man. That is how I knew to call for the physician."

Faith's jaw dropped. "That sounds nearly as incredulous as my story. Who would do such a thing? Or know even where to bring the painting?"

"Perhaps they assumed you would be travelling to Castleton. I am not entirely sure. We can speak more of it later, but for now, I want you to know that you are safe and no one is going to be coming after us."

She nodded, trying to take in all that Lord Ashford had told her before she returned to the room.

There was so much more to share, so many questions to ask and answers to provide.

But first, Eric had to come back to her.

She had no idea how she would continue on if he didn't.

"My lady?"

She looked up to find a maid had taken Lord Ashford's place in the doorway.

"I do not need anything," she said, waving the girl away.

"Before I go," the maid said, looking from one side to the other, "I have a suggestion for you."

She stepped into the room, holding out a bowl. Even from this distance, its foul smell had Faith leaning back away from it.

"My mother is a healer, and I have learned much from

her. I would suggest putting this on the wound. My mother swears that it will stop bleeding and prevent festering."

Faith eyed her skeptically. She wasn't much for witchcraft and such treatments, but at this point, she wasn't sure what other choice she had after the physician had left without any suggestion.

"Have you ever seen it work?" Faith asked.

"I have never seen it make anything worse, if that helps," the maid said with a small smile, placing the bowl beside the bed. If that smell didn't wake Eric, Faith wondered if anything ever would.

"Give it a try," the maid said. "If you need more, ask for me. My name is Jane."

Faith nodded her thanks, staring at Eric. She would do anything to make him well again.

Anything at all.

CHAPTER 26

*E*ric could sense light behind his eyes, but it took him a few tries before he could open them and see the room around him. His mouth was dry and there was a dull ache in his lower right leg – but he was alive.

He turned his head from one side to the other, trying to ascertain exactly where he was.

"Eric?"

He smelled her before he saw her, and then she was practically flying across the bed toward him, her body covering his.

"Faith?"

He lifted his arms, pleased to find that they still worked fine at least, before he wrapped them around her.

"Oof," he said as he took in her weight, and she was quickly pushing up and away from him.

"I am so sorry. I should not have done that. I am just so happy to see you awake and speaking and—"

He had so much to say, but each time he tried for more words, his voice cracked.

"Drink?" he managed, and she quickly went to his bedside and lifted water to his lips.

He lay his head back afterward, confused and needing to know what had happened. All that they had been through came rushing back to him, and he took a deep breath of relief that Faith was with him, however that had come about.

"You are not hurt?" he asked, scanning her body with his eyes.

"No, I am completely fine."

"They didn't do anything to you?"

"Nothing. Those men are not a threat anymore."

"Thank God," he said, closing his eyes for a moment in relief.

"How do you feel?" she asked.

"Alive."

"You were shot in the leg."

"That, I do recall," he said, managing a small smile.

"It appears that you have not lost your sense of humor."

"No, that you are stuck with."

He reached out, finding her hand and interlacing his fingers with hers.

"Will I lose the leg?" he asked.

His father had been a soldier. He was well aware of the likely outcome of a gunshot wound. Usually, it meant the loss of a limb, which often led to death if the initial wound hadn't caused it already. But he had enough resolve now to live – he had Faith.

"The physician didn't have much to say," Faith said. "Just that it took some of your muscle. If it begins to fester, we will call the surgeon."

A surgeon meant amputation – of that, Eric was well aware.

He nodded. "Very well." He wrinkled his nose. "What is that foul smell?"

"That," Faith said, "is a poultice from a healer. And I do believe that it has saved your life. Since we began applying it, you have improved."

"I have to say I am rather shocked you agreed to it."

Eric had heard of such things, but Faith was the last person he would ever guess who would believe in them.

"So was I," Faith said with a shrug. "But I figured nothing could hurt, and here we are."

He nodded.

"There is so much more to tell you," Faith said, sitting on the bed beside him and inching closer. "But first…" she took a breath and looked down at her hands. It was one of the first times he had ever seen her so nervous.

"It is just me, Faith," he said, tugging at her. "Nothing to be scared about."

She blew out the breath she had been holding and smiled somewhat tremulously.

"Yes, well that is the thing."

He waited, knowing that she was not one to back down – he just had to be patient.

"I love you," she finally said, her eyes lifting to meet his, a watery sheen in front of them. "I love you more than I ever wanted to love anyone. You are everything to me, and I was such a fool before. I was worried that you would leave me, worried that I would never be enough for you. But now, I almost lost you, and I never told you how I truly felt. The truth is, I am going to love you whether I want to or not. Whether you betray me or prefer another or even die on me – which you'd better not."

She let out an odd snort hiccup that almost had him laughing, but he knew that she would think he found her confession humorous so he held it in.

"As I sat here, staring at you, I finally realized that all I could do was tell you how I truly felt, and then you could do with that what you chose. My heart is yours."

Eric stared at her, drinking in her beauty and the trust she had just given to him – trust that he knew had been so difficult for her to part with.

"Faith," he said, reaching out and cupping her cheek in his hand. "I've loved you since the moment I saw you. I am sorry I ever betrayed you, but you know that I did not do so purposely. I am the luckiest man in the world to receive your love again, and I will not be fool enough to let that go. Sometimes I have a hard time finding my way in the world, but you... well, you are my compass."

She laughed at that through the tears in her eyes, leaning down toward him and nuzzling her head into his shoulder.

"Does this hurt?"

"No," he said. "How did Ashford take the news of the lost map?"

"Actually," Faith said, leaning up to look at him contemplatively, "that was the strangest thing..."

Eric could hardly believe the story she told him, and he was shaking his head by the time she finished.

"First the return of the necklace and now the map," he mused. "Someone out there is helping us – or Ashford. But who?"

"That's a good question, but not one that anyone appears to have an answer to," Faith said. "We were waiting until you were well enough to look at the map with the compass. Madeline is joining us soon to help Cassandra with the baby, and then I suppose it is time for us to go home."

Eric smiled at her, loving the way "home" rolled off of her tongue – especially when it meant the place they would live together.

"I can hardly wait," he said, hating how heavy his eyelids

had become, for all he wanted to do was stare at Faith and the love in her eyes that was looking back at him.

"That, however, can come later," she said. "You should sleep now."

"As you wish," he said, holding her close. "Stay with me?"

"Forever," she said, snuggling closer.

It was all he had ever wanted.

And this time, he would never let her go.

CHAPTER 27

It was another few days before Eric was healed enough to join the rest of the party, although managing his way around Castleton still took significant effort. The groundskeeper had made him a walking stick which did help considerably, although the pain was still obvious when he walked up and down the stairs.

Faith admired his determination to continue on and not complain, even though she knew he must be hurting tremendously.

"Ferrington, so glad to see you up and about," Lord Ashford said when he joined them in the drawing room. Cassandra, her husband Lord Covington, and Madeline were all there as well, and Faith sat on the sofa beside Eric, ready to help him with whatever he might need, although he waved her away.

"I am up, although not moving especially well," Eric said with a short laugh. "Feeling something of an invalid at the moment."

"But you're alive," Faith said quietly. "That is what matters the most."

Eric nodded. "From the looks of things, I should be able to keep the leg, although it will probably never be the same again. My adventures just might be over."

"You're married to Faith now," Madeline said with a mischievous grin. "Your adventures are just beginning."

They laughed at that before Ashford stepped forward, placing the map they had found in San Sebastian on the table in front of them.

"Before you return home I thought we should take a look at this together," Ashford said, lifting his eyebrows in question before smoothing out the edges. "I can tell from the terrain that this is likely Castleton, but I am having difficulty determining to where the map is pointing. Perhaps a fresh set of eyes will help."

"A fresh set of eyes," Eric said, pulling out the compass from his pocket and passing it to Ashford, "or by using this instrument."

Ashford's brow furrowed in confusion.

"That is the piece of necklace."

"It is," Eric said with a grin. "It is also a compass. A compass and an ocular device. It all fits together."

He passed the compass to Lord Ashford, who held it in his hands almost reverently before putting it up to his eye and staring at the map while the rest of them watched him, nearly holding their breath.

"It is not only a compass," Lord Ashford said with an inhale, "but it adds dimension to the map. I think this shows the way to the treasure."

There was more excitement in his voice than Faith had ever heard before, and Cassandra sat for just a moment before her anticipation was obviously no longer able to be contained and she stood and walked over to her brother, waiting impatiently until he was finished before taking the compass from him and looking through it herself.

"That's incredible," she breathed after looking for a few moments before lifting her eyes to stare at her brother. "Oh, Gideon, I can hardly believe it. We're finally going to recover all that we have been searching for."

"As long as the Spaniards do not get there first," he said darkly.

"Have we heard what happened to *Don* Raphael?" Faith asked, trying not to allow the rest of them to see her concern. She had been saved from the men, yes, but that didn't mean that she wasn't fearful that they might catch her unaware, without her weapons this time. She couldn't walk around wearing her bow and arrows.

"We have, as it happens," Lord Ashford said. "I heard from the magistrate that *Don* Raphael and his men were delivered to London and put into prison until it is decided what to do with them."

"Prison?" Faith said, surprised. "Are we certain that they will not find a way to be released? *Don* Raphael is a nobleman."

"A nobleman in Spain – not England," Lord Ashford said. "He tried to abduct the daughter of an earl. Your father, Lady Ferrington, has been very much involved in ensuring that *Don* Raphael pays for what he has done."

"My goodness," Faith murmured. "I had no idea."

"It took some time for word to arrive to us," Lord Ashford said. "I didn't want to concern you with it until we were sure that Ferrington, here, had recovered."

"I should send word to my brother," Eric murmured. "He will likely be concerned."

"We have already done so," Ashford said. "He asked if he should return but I told him that I would write if anything changed for the worse. We were most hopeful that it would only be for the better."

"And here we are," Faith said. "Thank you for providing your hospitality while Eric recovers."

Ashford laughed. "After all that you have done and being injured in trying to help me? It is the least that I could do. Once we find the treasure, then I—"

Eric held up his hand. "You will do nothing. The treasure is yours. We are only along for the fun of it all." He looked over at Faith. "I think we are ready to return home now."

"You do not want to stay and see what happens next?" Ashford said, surprise on his face. "This could be quite the end to the adventure."

"If you need anything, we are but a letter away," Eric said. "We shall leave you to find this treasure and be on our way tomorrow as we eagerly await news of your discovery."

"Well, then," Ashford said, looking around the room, "we best make the most of tonight. Anyone interested in a glass of brandy?"

They all knew the answer to that question.

CHAPTER 28

Faith had never been to Eric's family home.

She had visited their London house and, of course, the estate where his brother and Percy had married, but never here. It was not as though their parents were friends, and Faith could see why now after the exchange between their mothers at the wedding breakfast.

"My goodness," she said, standing in front of the vast estate made of finely cut, polished stone. They had travelled up a long, winding driveway, through manicured gardens and rolling landscapes until the carriage came to a stop in front of the grand portico supported by imposing columns.

The entrance, flanked by large windows, was open, the house perfectly symmetrical as long wings flew out to each side of the main building.

After having disembarked from the carriage to find the staff fanned out and waiting for them, Faith shifted from one foot to the other when Eric's mother stood in the entrance, perfectly framed on all sides.

"There you are," the previous Lady Ferrington said, hurrying down the stairs. "I have been waiting for days."

"Good to see you, Mother," Eric said, hobbling forward, kissing her on the cheek, but she quickly drew away from him the moment she noticed the change in his gait.

"My word, what happened to you?" she asked, looking down. Eric tried to laugh it off at first but sighed when he realized his mother wasn't having it.

"It is quite the story," he said. "Why do we not go inside and I shall tell you all about it?"

"Very well," his mother said, holding her arm out, apparently believing that Eric was going to escort her in.

"Mother," Eric said without criticism, "we shall wait until Faith is ready."

"Of course," his mother said, dipping her head, and Faith smiled at her, wanting to set things right from the start.

"It is wonderful to see you," she said. "Thank you for looking after everything while you awaited us."

"I shall do all I can to make you comfortable," his mother said as the three of them began the slow walk up the stairs, one of the footmen having recognized the situation and striding forward to offer his assistance to Eric. "I have moved my things out of the lady of the house's bedchamber. I was not sure exactly where to move them as of yet. If you would prefer that I move to the dower house, I am happy to do so."

Faith's chest warmed at the dowager countess' show of kindness, and she placed her hand on her arm.

"We would be happy to have you remain in the house with us," she said, looking around her. "From what I can see there are more than enough rooms."

"I appreciate that," Eric's mother said quietly. "I do not wish to make anything difficult for you, but know that whatever you need, I am there for you."

"Thank you," Faith said. "I am sure that I shall need some help transitioning to the lady of the house."

She caught Eric's warm smile as they continued inside,

and after providing his mother with a version of the story that included the highwaymen but not that they had been chased from Spain, they eventually retired after their long day of travel.

Faith made for her bedroom when Eric held out a hand to stop her.

"Where do you think you are going?"

"To my chamber to undress," she said, but he shook his head with a wicked grin.

"Our bedrooms might be attached, but tonight you will start with me. I think I became rather adept at undressing you during our travels."

Faith allowed him to pull her in close to him. "Oh my, what will the servants think?"

"Let them think whatever they choose," he said. "We are the lord and lady of the house. We can do as we please."

She grinned at that, and together they entered his room. Faith could tell that he was trying not to lean on her as he hobbled in. They had not come together since his shooting, and while Faith had missed him, she worried that he might aggravate the injury.

"Why do you look nervous?" he asked.

"I'm not nervous," she said even as a tremor shook through her. "I am worried about you. And, I'll admit, excited."

"Oh, my lady," he said, "There is nothing for you to worry about. I have been looking forward to this more than you could ever imagine."

"Show me?" she murmured, and he nodded, his smile wicked.

"With pleasure."

"Perhaps you should lie down first so that I do not hurt you," she said, and he grabbed her shoulders and looked her in the eye.

"Faith," he said firmly. "If anything hurts, I shall tell you. But until then, we enjoy each other and do not worry about any wound I might have. Understand?"

"Do you promise you will say something if you are hurting?"

"I promise."

"Very well," she said, her heart beginning to beat rapidly at the thought of being with him again. "Do you need some help?"

"With what?"

"Undressing."

"On one condition."

"Which is?"

"That you do so only as part of seducing me and *not* because you think I am insufficient in any way."

"Oh, Eric," she said, shaking her head. "You could be unable to walk altogether and you could never be insufficient. You must realize that you are more than the strong, unbreakable lord that you want everyone to think you are. You are more worthy than any other man I've ever met before. And I thank you for showing me that part of you."

She stepped forward, lifting her hand and sliding it down his cheek as she stared into his eyes.

When they had first come together, it had been so passionate, so fiery, and while Faith knew that passion would always remain between them, she was now swept up in an emotion unlike any she had ever felt before. One that was tender, raw, vulnerable.

It no longer scared her, as it would have just a few months ago. Instead, her trust in Eric had grown so deep that she knew she would always be safe, as long as he was there beside her.

He leaned in, his large hand cupping the back of her head in one possessive move as he kissed her deeply, drinking her in, reminding her that she was his forever now. His other arm was strong around her back, and Faith knew he was likely wishing that he could pick her up and lift her onto the bed.

Instead, she backed up toward it herself, pressing one more kiss upon his lips before she turned around and presented her back to him.

"I believe someone promised he would be my lady's maid tonight?" she said, her eyebrows wiggling slightly, and he chuckled heartily against her neck, his hands sliding over her sides.

"As my lady commands," he said as he took his time undressing her, his fingers moving slowly as he untied the laces that held her bodice together, the soft pads of his thumbs grazing over her back, causing her to shiver.

Faith let out a soft sigh of pleasure, her eyes falling closed as she tilted her head back, exposing her neck to invite his soft kisses that she loved so much as he slid the sleeves of her gown off of her arms.

As he worked on layer after layer, his touch sent sparks throughout Faith's body. She was so lost in him and all that surrounded them here in this bedroom that she nearly forgot a world outside of it existed.

His fingers trailed down her spine, causing shivers as he went until he reached the small of her back. She let out a soft gasp, to which he chuckled and pushed her dress over her hips until it pooled at her feet.

Faith stepped out of it, now clad only in her thin chemise. She slowly turned around, her eyes locking onto Eric's, which were staring at her in hunger.

He was already shirtless himself, his strong, chiselled chest and abdomen waiting for her.

Eric stepped closer, his hands cupping Faith's cheeks as he leaned in and kissed her deeply once more. She melted into him as his hands travelled over her body until he deftly released the ribbon on her chemise and the fabric floated away, leaving her bare before him.

Reaching forward, she untied the fall of his breeches herself, shifting so that he could hold onto the bed if needed while he pulled them off.

Eric's strong hands gripped the wooden bedpost as he lifted himself onto the mattress. Faith followed, crawling over toward him on hands and knees as he lay back and waited for her to join him.

With a sultry smile, she straddled him, placing her hands on his broad chest as she leaned forward to kiss him again.

Eric's fingers traced the curves of her breasts and hips and as their mouths moved together, Faith moaned, her hands roaming over his chest and down his abdomen. His arousal pressed into her thigh, and she was suddenly desperate for it – for him. Eric must have felt the same, for he pulled back away from the kiss, his lips now moving down her neck, nibbling gently on her collarbone. He took one of her nipples into his mouth, sucking until she was writhing above him, desperate for more.

She wriggled down his body and he leaned on his elbows, watching her with hooded eyes as she dipped her head and lifted his cock with her mouth, teasing it with her tongue, satisfaction growing warm in her chest when he groaned in response.

Faith would never have thought that she would enjoy taking a man in her mouth, but she loved the power that came with it, the opportunity to provide him with all of the satisfaction she could give.

Finally, he leaned down, reaching for her, sliding her back over his body and lifting her until she was sitting right over top of him. One of his hands slipped between them and he rubbed her slowly, making sure she was ready for him until he nodded in satisfaction and released her.

Gripping his shoulders, she held herself above him until she slid down slowly as he notched within her. She paused, giving herself a moment to adjust.

How had she gone so many years without his touch? It had only been a few weeks since he had been injured and it felt like forever since they had been together like this.

"What is wrong?" he asked, leaning up on his elbows so that he could see her.

"I am afraid that I will hurt you."

"What did we say about that?" he asked, bopping her on the nose with his index finger. "You are perfect. Do not hold back on my account."

She sunk deeper, relaxing around him until he was fully seated within her. She took a breath, becoming used to his size as she was so full, so complete when they were together. She looked into his eyes and could tell that he felt the same as he leaned up and captured her mouth with his.

Eric shifted and found one of her nipples again, this time with his mouth while his hands moved to her hips, helping her move, the slow love play not vanishing but becoming more urgent, more desperate, as their bodies rocked together as one.

Eric suddenly surged up off of the bed, lifting Faith and moving her beside him. She started in surprise, staring up at him as his normally bright and cheerful demeanor was replaced with a man intent on achieving his aim.

"Eric, what are—"

"On your knees," he murmured, not entirely commanding but not asking either. There was still tenderness in his tone, but Faith didn't mind being ordered about – in bed. Nowhere else.

She did as he instructed, perching on her knees, and he

THE LORD'S COMPASS

reached out, one of his hands sliding her legs wider apart before kneeling between her thighs.

Faith bit her lip before the words emerged, words that would ask him if he was sure he should be doing this. She had a feeling that he was likely causing a great risk of injury to his leg, but to ask him now would only mean that he would feel he must further prove that he was the same man he had always been.

He wrapped his arm around Faith, sliding his fingers into her very center, rocking her back and forth against them.

"You're so ready for me," he murmured in her ear before smacking her bottom – not hard, but enough to make her start – and burn for him even more.

"Eric, if you do not hurry up and finish what you started, then I'll—I'll—"

"You will what?" he asked, dark humor in his tone.

"I will ask my mother to come stay with us."

That had him moving.

He slid further into her, stretching her, filling her again, until he pushed forward all the way, murmuring her name in supplication.

"Faith," he groaned out, and she answered him, pushing back against him until there was nowhere left for him to go.

He pulled out slightly, then back in again, each thrust becoming faster, deeper, as he hit a place within her that she didn't even know existed. She wasn't ready when the waves of light began pulsing through her body, and she cried his name out so loudly it was a wonder the plethora of servants in this house didn't come running to make sure she was all right.

After another moment, he went rigid behind her, and then he was pulsing inside of her, spending deep within as his hands grasped her hips and he rocked in tiny motions against her until he collapsed over top of her, holding himself up just enough that she didn't receive all of his weight.

She turned over, flat on the bed beneath them, catching his head to her chest as she flung her arm over her eyes.

They lay like that for minutes, no words needed as they basked in the love they had shared. Faith brushed her fingers through his silky hair, sliding it off his brow as she took in the bedchamber around her, which she hadn't considered before as she had been... distracted.

They were lying upon a massive bed, velvet draperies hanging around them as the marble fireplace with its hearty fire cast light upon what appeared to be royal blue walls and caused the gold accents around the room to glimmer.

It was a large room, with a writing desk, a dressing table, a wardrobe, and a sitting area with a table and two rather comfortable-looking chairs.

Her bedroom was nearly matching, only with daintier furniture and lilac walls.

"What are you thinking about?" Eric asked, looking up at her, and she smiled down at him.

"I am thinking about my home now. Here, with you."

"I hope there is nowhere else you would rather be."

She paused for a moment before answering.

"It's funny," she mused. "I always thought that I would be happiest living alone, without a man to answer to or rely on. Then you came along. When I caught you in an embrace, I quickly thought the worst. But perhaps I was just looking for an excuse, because I was scared, for so many reasons. Now, here we are, and I cannot imagine life any other way."

He leaned up, kissing her before pillowing his chin on his hands.

"I have a hard time finding my way sometimes, Faith," he said. "But you will always show me the right path. You are the direction I never knew I needed. My compass."

"I love you, Lord Ferrington."

"And I love you, Lady Ferrington."

"Do you know where you are going now?"

"Anywhere," he said with a grin, "As long as I am with you."

EPILOGUE

"Faith? Where are you?"

Faith had just finished dressing for the day when she heard Eric's boisterous call coming from outside her bedchamber.

"Nothing further," she told her maid with a smile before going to the door, not attempting to contain the bounce in her step that Eric's voice caused.

"I'm here," she said, stepping outside the door to find Eric waiting, a grin on his face even larger than usual.

"I have a gift for you," he said, his hands behind his back.

"A gift?" she said with raised brows. "We only just returned last week and I don't need anything."

"That is where you are wrong," he said. "I do believe you need this."

She eyed him suspiciously. She wasn't exactly one for surprises, but he was so eager that she couldn't help but catch some of his excitement.

"Very well," she said, waving her hand out. "What is it?"

"You must follow me," he said, reaching out to clasp her

hand, surprising her for she had guessed that he had held something in his hands.

She allowed him to lead her through the estate, down the stairs and into the library, out through the terrace doors. Eric had their cloaks prepared, and she followed him through the immaculate gardens. He stopped a few times, muttering to himself before turning one way and then the other.

"Are you lost?" she asked, trying to contain her mirth.

"Of course not," he said. "This is my home."

"Of course," she said, but when he stopped and turned again, she was unable to contain her laughter. He answered her with a small smile of his own.

"Very well," he said. "I might be slightly lost."

She laughed aloud, shaking her head, until finally, he pulled her through the hedge into a clearing.

"Here we are!" he said triumphantly, and Faith's jaw dropped open.

For in front of them was a beautiful, intricate, archery course, and there, sitting across from the field of targets that awaited, was a fine new quiver of arrows and the most beautiful bow Faith had ever seen.

"Oh, Eric," she said, bringing a hand to her mouth as she walked over, sinking to her knees, uncaring about any stains that might be left on her dress. "This is gorgeous."

She removed her gloves and ran her hand over the fine wood of the bow before placing the quiver on her back. She reached back, drew out an arrow, and notched it onto the bow before lining up to face her target.

She closed an eye, aimed, and let the arrow fly. It landed in the middle of the target with a *thud* that had her smiling and Eric clapping proudly.

He walked toward her, a knowing grin on his face.

"What do you think? Do you enjoy the gift?"

"It is amazing," she said, reaching her arms out and wrapping them around his neck. "I had missed time with my bow and arrows. Thank you for knowing exactly what I needed to truly make this feel like home."

She leaned in, tilting her head up to his and meeting his lips, their kiss tender and giving. Faith sank into him, wondering if they should risk exploring one another further here within the best gift she had ever received when a voice broke through her musings.

"My lord! My lady!"

They parted at the sound of one of the footmen running toward them. When he cleared the break in the trees and came into view, they could see that he was holding a letter outstretched before him.

"What is it, Jones?" Eric asked, leaving Faith's side and meeting him halfway.

"An urgent message," the footman said through heavy breaths. "It was sent by a messenger on horseback who said you needed to receive it at once."

Eric and Faith exchanged a look of concern before Eric tore into it, Faith impatiently ducking under his arm so that she could read it at the same time as him. She finished the note quicker than he did, unable to prevent the gasp that emerged. She knew when Eric read the same as his hands tightened around her upper arms.

"When did this arrive?" Eric demanded.

"Just a few minutes ago," the footman said, and Faith grabbed Eric's arm.

"It is dated a week ago," she said. "Oh, Eric, what should we do? Should we stay here and search in the area, as Lord Ashford asks, or should we return to Castleton and try to help coordinate the search from there?"

"I know she is one of your closest friends, and the most

important thing is that you are not put into any danger yourself," he said, holding up a hand when Faith began to protest. "I am not saying that is by staying here. We will decide what is best – together."

Faith took a deep breath, trying to calm her nerves. "I can hardly believe this is happening."

"We will get her back, Faith," he said. "I know we will."

She read the note one more time to make sure that she wasn't in the midst of some nightmare.

But no. Madeline was gone. Disappeared from Castleton. And no one had any idea where she might be.

THE END

* * *

Dear reader,

Thank you for taking this journey with Eric and Faith from England to Spain and back again! I hope you enjoyed their story and continued quest for the treasure.

Next is the fifth and final book of the series, The Heir's Fortune! It brings us around full circle to complete this story. Will our heroes and heroines find the treasure? Will Gideon and Madeline find love? You can find a sneak peek in the pages after this one or preorder here: The Heir's Fortune!

If you haven't yet signed up for my newsletter, I would love to have you join! You will receive a free book, as well as links to giveaways, sales, new releases, and stories about my coffee addiction, my struggle to keep my plants alive, and how much trouble one loveable wolf lookalike dog can get into.

www.elliestclair.com/ellies-newsletter

You will also receive links to giveaways, sales, updates, launch information, promos, and the newest recommended reads.

Or you can join my Facebook group, Ellie St. Clair's Ever Afters, and stay in touch daily.

Happy reading!

Ellie

* * *

The Heir's Fortune
The Reckless Rogues, Book 5

SHE NEVER THOUGHT she would need a knight-in-shining-armor – most especially in the form of her best friend's brother.

Despite the scandals that plague his family, future duke Lord Gideon Sutcliffe vows to restore the dukedom's reputation and refill its coffers. His two solutions? Finding the treasure he's been hunting, or marrying for a worthwhile dowry.

Neither of which includes Lady Madeline Bainbridge. With a paltry dowry, average looks, a forthright, dramatic manner, and a penchant for all things Gothic, she is the last woman Gideon would need. Nor does his straightforward, responsible manner match her reckless ways.

When Madeline is kidnapped by those determined to reclaim the treasure, it will be a race to see who rescues her first – Gideon or herself. When they begin to see that there is more to one another than they initially assumed, will the mismatched pair escape unscathed and find the treasure, or does fortune have another ending in store?

This is best-friend's-brother, opposites attract, he-falls-first Regency romance featuring a gothic-loving heroine and a dutiful future duke. The Reckless Rogues series is best read in order.

THE HEIR'S FORTUNE - CHAPTER ONE

"Come on out, now, no need to be shy."

Gideon stretched his hand as far as he could as while using the other to try to inch himself forward, but it was no use – he wasn't going to fit in the hollowed-out tree trunk that lay across the path of the ruins before him.

The dog at the other end whimpered and shrunk away from him, still shivering. Gideon sighed as he let his arm go limp, wishing he had an enticing piece of food on him to draw the dog out, but, alas, the dog found him as unremarkable as everyone else did.

"I promise if you come with me, I will take you to the kitchen, and the Cook will give you all of the scrap meat you'd like. I cannot say it will be particularly well-prepared, but you do not have high standards, do you now?"

The dog, either a pup or a small breed, Gideon couldn't tell from where he was, tilted its head to the side, one ear flopping over as though he was listening to him and considering his words.

"I cannot leave you out here but I am becoming rather chilled," Gideon said, holding his hand out again, palm up, and the dog leaned its head forward, sniffing. "There we go—"

"What are you doing?"

Gideon jumped, the voice startling him, causing him to hit his head on the top of the log.

"Damn it," he said, lifting a hand to the sore spot, as the dog whimpered and drew away from him once more.

He shuffled backward now, squinting up to see the figure towering over him in front of the now-setting sun, arms crossed over her chest as her cloak billowed in the cold wind behind her.

"Lady Madeline?" he said, trying to contain his groan as he rubbed his head. "You startled me."

"Clearly," she said, looking around. "I almost passed by you, but I must admit that my curiosity as to why a future duke was on his belly, crawling into a log in the middle of the forest was just too overwhelming to continue on without learning more. Please, you must explain."

"So that you can tell this story to our friends for your amusement?" he snorted. "I think not."

"I shall be telling it one way or another, so you might as well provide me with your side of things."

"Fine," he said, opening his mouth to explain his dilemma, but just as he did, a whine resounded.

"What was that?" Lady Madeline asked, looking from one side to the other, her silky dark hair that had fallen out of most of its pins floating around her face.

"That," Gideon said with exasperation, "is what I am trying to save."

She fixed with him a hard stare, but instead of demanding more information or leaving at the idea of a wild animal as most women would, she rounded the other side of the log, crouching down without care that her knee was resting on the damp ground before standing with the puppy in her arms, despite its dirty and matted soft fur against her cloak and gown underneath.

"Is this who you were trying so hard to catch?" she asked as she nuzzled her face against the dog's fur.

"Yes," Gideon said, unable to mask his annoyance as he stood, brushing dirt and dried leaves off of his breeches. "Two people being here made it much easier."

"Or maybe he just likes me better," Madeline said with a grin before lifting the puppy in front of her to inspect him. "Who is he?"

"I am not sure," Gideon said, lifting his hands to the side. "I was walking around the ruins and heard a noise so I came to investigate. That's when I found him."

"I see," she said. "My best guess is that he is a couple of months old, which means he is old enough to have left his mama but I wouldn't say could survive long on his own."

"I doubt it," Gideon said, stepping forward toward Lady Madeline and the dog. She was his sister's closest friend and had spent a great deal of time at Castleton, and yet, he didn't know her very well. She was so forward and apt to say the most unlikely comments that he always avoided her if he could, for she made him feel on edge.

He reached out a hand and hesitantly ran it down the dog's soft fur, surprised when the puppy leaned into his touch with a whimper.

Lady Madeline looked up at him in surprise, and a tremble ran down Gideon's spine at her proximity. A tremble from... uneasiness? He never knew what to expect from this woman – and he did not like surprises.

"Maybe he doesn't mind you so much after all," she said with a laugh as the puppy licked his hand. "What were you doing out here, anyway?"

"Seeing to my lands," he said guardedly, uncertain why he needed to have an excuse to wander his own property.

"You weren't searching for treasure?" she asked with a sly smile over the dog's head.

"Would it matter if I was?" he asked defensively. "I have every right to do so."

"Steady there, I was just asking," she said with what seemed to be a roll of her eyes. "Do you take everything so seriously?"

"Everything that matters," he said, watching her black cloak swirl in the wind. "We should be getting back. The sun is lowering."

"What about the dog?" she asked, lifting the bundle in her arms, and he crooked his fingers toward her.

"I'll take him."

She stepped backward so that they were both out of reach, fixing him with a hard stare. "Where are you going to take him?"

"To the stables," he said. "Where would you think I would take him?"

She bit her lip, her normally stoic façade loosening its grip, allowing him to see a different side of her.

"He's so small and has been out here all alone," she said. "Do you not think he should come to the house?"

Gideon took a breath, lifting a hand in the air. "He chose to come to you, so I suppose you can do with him what you'd like."

She was already shaking her head. "I cannot have a dog."

"Why not?"

She shrugged her shoulders. "I am not one to make much commitment to anything. I cannot keep a dog when I do not know where I might be living in a short time."

Gideon cocked his head to the side as he stared at the two of them. "He doesn't seem to understand that."

Nor did Gideon, but he wasn't about to ask questions. Madeline looked down at the dog, a moment of vulnerability crossing over her face before she shoved the dog toward him. "Here," she said. "Take him. He's yours."

Gideon softened, seeing how much this had affected her.

"I'll take him to the stables, but only to be cleaned up, and then he can come inside," he said. "We shall see what my mother thinks of him."

"Of course," Lady Madeline said, giving her head a curt nod. "I should be going."

"I will walk you back," he said. "You shouldn't be out here alone."

"I shouldn't," she said. "But I am anyway."

And with that, she strode off, fast enough to make him aware that she would prefer he did not follow.

She was a mystery that one. But one mystery that wasn't up to him to solve.

* * *

Try as he might to concentrate on anything other than Lady Madeline, she was still on his mind when Cassandra found him in his study a short time later – the dog at his feet curled up on a pillow that had previously been perched upon one of the parlor sofas. He hoped his mother wouldn't note its absence, or, if she did, she would forgive him. She was currently upstairs visiting with his father and had yet to take any note of the dog.

"Oh, there he is!"

Gideon looked up at his sister's voice, surprised that she was so excited to see him, but when she ran in to crouch beside the dog, he realized that she wasn't talking to him at all. She reached down to let the puppy lick her face.

"Where is your baby?" Gideon asked, more curious than perturbed. Since the young lad had been born, Cassandra had spent far more time with the baby than most other women of her station would with their offspring. Gideon actually admired her for it.

"He's with Madeline," she said, and Gideon found himself rather piqued at her friend's name, but before he could ask any more, Devon – Lord Covington, Cassandra's husband, and Gideon's closest friend – followed his wife in the door.

"I heard there was a pup in here," he said, looking around the room. "Has he made a mess all over the floor yet?"

"Not yet," Gideon said. "A footman has seen to his requirements."

"Good to hear it," Devon said with a grin. "Perhaps you will make a proud papa after all."

Gideon snorted, bending his head so that Devon and Cassandra wouldn't see his face. Despite being closer to him than any other two people in the world, he didn't want them to see how much the words affected him.

For it was true – he *would* like to be a father. He just wasn't sure if and when that day would ever come.

"It is unfortunate that Hope, Faith, Percy, and their husbands have left," Cassandra said as she stroked the dog, whose fur was rather soft now that it had been properly washed. "They would have loved him."

"I'd like to see Whitehall with a dog," Covington said with a laugh, referencing the rather ill-natured Lord Whitehall, who had married Lady Hope.

The five men who had been part of their group that undertook daring adventures had joined him on this quest when he had found a riddle that he assumed would lead to a treasure. His sister had found another copy of the same riddle, leading her and her four closest friends to start their own hunt. Eventually, they merged their efforts after Cassandra and Covington fell in love while solving the first riddle, which had only led to another clue instead of the treasure Gideon had been hoping for.

"Whitehall might be a genius codebreaker, which helped us a great deal when it came to solving the second clue, but an animal man, I cannot see," Gideon said, leaning back, no longer attempting the pretense of continuing his work.

The code Whitehall had solved with the help of Hope had led to a third clue, one which required retrieving a necklace from Gideon and Cassandra's aunt in Bath. As Lady Percy was there at the same time as Noah Rowley, they had undertaken the search together, which ended in finding a clue within the necklace – and marriage to one another.

Rowley's brother, Lord Ferrington, had then traveled to Spain along with a stowaway, Lady Faith, and they had returned with a map as well as a marriage due to their compromising situation. Fortunately, it had led to love in the end.

As for the map? Gideon now had it in his possession.

"What were you doing in the ruins, anyway?" Cassandra asked. "The last time we were there, Devon knocked over a wall and we were both nearly injured."

"But aren't you glad we were?" Devon asked, grinning suggestively at his wife, which had Gideon leaning back in his chair and shaking his head.

"I was getting impatient," he said. "I know we need to take a better look at the map together and solve the path it will be leading us down, but I couldn't help the urge to begin searching myself."

"That's how you will get in trouble, Gideon," Cassandra said, straightening. "All of us who have gone after a clue have found ourselves in danger at one time or another."

"Is that why you are still here?" Gideon asked with sinking dread in his stomach. "I wondered why you hadn't left yet. I had assumed that you wanted to stay to see this through, but is it because you do not think I am capable of accomplishing this alone?"

"Of course you are more than capable," Cassandra said, rising from the floor where the dog had returned to his slumber and taking a chair in front of his desk, crossing her arms over her chest. "We are still here for a few reasons. One being that I wanted Mother to be able to spend time with the baby."

"And we do want to see this thing through, that part is true. We started this and we would like to see it to the finish," Devon added, exchanging a meaningful look with his wife.

"And also…" Cassandra said, slightly wincing as she did so, "We hate to see you all alone."

"Mother and Father are both here, and I have been alone for years," Gideon said, his spine straightening. "I am more than capable of looking after myself."

"You can look after yourself, but do you want to?" Cassandra asked imploringly. "No one *wants* to be alone."

"Some of us have to be happy doing so," he said uncomfortably, for his statement was not entirely true.

"Will you not seek out a wife?" she asked, shifting forward in her seat, her blue eyes boring into him.

"In due time," Gideon said, exasperated with this conversation, but he did feel that it owed it to the two people closer to him than any other in the world to explain his thoughts. "I cannot offer a woman marriage when we live in such ruins."

"Castleton is hardly a ruin," Devon said, leaning back against the doorframe as he studied him. Devon had helped Gideon through some difficult times in his life, and likely knew what he was thinking better than anyone. "Yes, it could use some improvements, but when I tell you that it is comfortable and I enjoy my time here, I mean it."

"We need servants, we need improvements, we need furniture that wasn't built for my great-grandfather!" Gideon said, throwing his hands into the air. "I'd like to offer a woman more than this. I have rested my hopes on this treasure for over a year now. However... if this treasure comes to nothing — and I am beginning to think it might not — then I might have less choice as to who I marry."

"What is that supposed to mean?" Cassandra asked, her head snapping up, and she had to push back a piece of hair the same chestnut color as his own away from her face.

"It means," he said carefully, "that if there is no other option, I will have to marry a woman with a significant dowry."

Cassandra bit her lip. "Gideon, that is so sad."

He shrugged. "It's practical."

"Yes, but—"

"It is what it is, Cassandra," he said, not wanting to speak on it any longer.

"You know, I had always wondered if maybe Madeline—"

"No," he said swiftly, holding up a hand.

"Why would you not even entertain the idea?" she asked defensively, which made sense, for Cassandra was as loyal of a friend as there ever was.

"Madeline's family would want nothing to do with the scandals that come with ours."

"How can you say that?" Cassandra said indignantly. "For one, you just finished saying that you will marry for a fortune if you have to."

"Of which, if I am not mistaken, Madeline has none."

"Yes, but if we find the treasure, that doesn't matter. Why would you be willing to saddle another unsuspecting young woman with our family scandal and not Madeline?"

Gideon knew that his words were not going to be accepted by Cassandra, but he owed her the truth.

"Madeline is not the type of woman to sit back and allow scandal to ebb away."

"What does that mean?"

"It means... that she has a propensity to say what she

thinks without worrying about the consequences. I would like to lead our family back to respectability."

"That is a most terrible thing to say," Cassandra said, standing abruptly. "But perhaps I forgot the lengths you are willing to go to in order to make things so respectable."

"Cassandra…"

Cassandra just glared at him, and Gideon was reminded of how angry she had been with him for so many years. He had made mistakes in his past – mistakes that had led to her being ostracized for sins that she didn't even commit – and he thought they had moved past them.

But perhaps she had forgiven him but not forgotten.

"Well," Cassandra said, stepping backward toward Devon, who appeared rather ill-at-ease, caught between his wife and his closest friend, "whatever you do, do not let Mother or Father know of your plan. They would be devastated."

"Why?" Gideon said, raking a hand through his hair. "It is their fault we are in this mess."

"Gideon!"

He sighed, lowering his head. "I know. That was a beastly thing to say. It was not the fault of either of them."

"No, it certainly was not," Cassandra said.

"It was my fault," Gideon muttered in a low voice, admitting out loud for the first time the thought that had haunted him for years now. "All of it. That is why I care so much, you know. Why I have been so determined to fix this. After Father became sick and the stewards and men of business began squandering all of the family's fortunes, I should have known. I should have been paying more attention, and spending more time at home. Then I would have realized that all was not right. But no, I was away at school, then spending time in London, having fun with my friends, playing a few pranks to release my boredom."

He waved his hand toward Devon, who looked as shocked as Cassandra.

"You cannot blame yourself for that," Devon said in a low voice. "You were doing what every young man of the *ton* does."

"That doesn't make it right," Gideon said. "If you don't mind, I will finish the rest of the accounts for the day before joining you for dinner."

"But—" Cassandra began, stepping forward, but Devon stopped her, gently placing his large hand over hers, lowering them down as he wrapped his other arm around her shoulders and began to steer her out the door.

"Let's leave Gideon be for a time, love."

"I'm not sure—"

"Go," Gideon said lowly as he sunk back into his chair. "Please."

As they walked out the door, arms around one another, Gideon had never felt so alone.

* * *

Keep reading The Heir's Fortune!

ALSO BY ELLIE ST. CLAIR

Reckless Rogues
The Earls's Secret
The Viscount's Code
The Scholar's Key
The Lord's Compass
The Heir's Fortune

The Remingtons of the Regency
The Mystery of the Debonair Duke
The Secret of the Dashing Detective
The Clue of the Brilliant Bastard
The Quest of the Reclusive Rogue

The Unconventional Ladies
Lady of Mystery
Lady of Fortune
Lady of Providence
Lady of Charade

The Unconventional Ladies Box Set

To the Time of the Highlanders
A Time to Wed
A Time to Love
A Time to Dream

Thieves of Desire

The Art of Stealing a Duke's Heart

A Jewel for the Taking

A Prize Worth Fighting For

Gambling for the Lost Lord's Love

Romance of a Robbery

Thieves of Desire Box Set

The Bluestocking Scandals

Designs on a Duke

Inventing the Viscount

Discovering the Baron

The Valet Experiment

Writing the Rake

Risking the Detective

A Noble Excavation

A Gentleman of Mystery

The Bluestocking Scandals Box Set: Books 1-4

The Bluestocking Scandals Box Set: Books 5-8

Blooming Brides

A Duke for Daisy

A Marquess for Marigold

An Earl for Iris

A Viscount for Violet

The Blooming Brides Box Set: Books 1-4

Happily Ever After

The Duke She Wished For
Someday Her Duke Will Come
Once Upon a Duke's Dream
He's a Duke, But I Love Him
Loved by the Viscount
Because the Earl Loved Me

Happily Ever After Box Set Books 1-3
Happily Ever After Box Set Books 4-6

The Victorian Highlanders
Duncan's Christmas - (prequel)
Callum's Vow
Finlay's Duty
Adam's Call
Roderick's Purpose
Peggy's Love

The Victorian Highlanders Box Set Books 1-5

Searching Hearts
Duke of Christmas (prequel)
Quest of Honor
Clue of Affection
Hearts of Trust
Hope of Romance
Promise of Redemption

Searching Hearts Box Set (Books 1-5)

Standalones

Always Your Love
The Stormswept Stowaway
A Touch of Temptation
Unmasking a Duke

Christmas Books
A Match Made at Christmas
A Match Made in Winter

Christmastide with His Countess
Her Christmas Wish
Merry Misrule
Duke of Christmas
Duncan's Christmas

For a full list of all of Ellie's books, please see www.elliestclair.com/books.

ABOUT THE AUTHOR

Ellie has always loved reading, writing, and history. For many years she has written short stories, non-fiction, and has worked on her true love and passion -- romance novels.

In every era there is the chance for romance, and Ellie enjoys exploring many different time periods, cultures, and geographic locations. No matter when or where, love can always prevail. She has a particular soft spot for the bad boys of history, and loves a strong heroine in her stories.

Ellie and her husband love nothing more than spending time at home with their children and Husky cross. Ellie can typically be found at the lake in the summer, pushing the stroller all year round, and, of course, with her computer in her lap or a book in hand.

She also loves corresponding with readers, so be sure to contact her!

> www.elliestclair.com
> ellie@elliestclair.com

- facebook.com/elliestclairauthor
- x.com/ellie_stclair
- instagram.com/elliestclairauthor
- amazon.com/author/elliestclair
- goodreads.com/elliestclair
- bookbub.com/authors/elliest.clair
- pinterest.com/elliestclair

Printed by Amazon Italia Logistica S.r.l.
Torrazza Piemonte (TO), Italy